William Shakespeare's Richard III: A Retelling in Prose

David Bruce

Published by David Bruce, 2022.

This is a work of fiction. Similarities to real people, places, or events are entirely coincidental.

WILLIAM SHAKESPEARE'S RICHARD III: A RETELLING IN PROSE

First edition. July 28, 2022.

Copyright © 2022 David Bruce.

ISBN: 979-8201112608

Written by David Bruce.

Table of Contents

Dedication

DEDICATED TO MY SISTER MARTHA

Martha wrote, "When I was working at Longaberger, I worked with a girl who had two children and was in the middle of a divorce. She was so worried about Christmas for her boys. I received a very nice Christmas bonus that year, and I went to my boss and started a donation fund for the girl. My boss told me later that she — my boss —delivered the money to the girl's mother and father and told them not to tell her who brought the money for her. Months later the girl told me that the boys had the best Christmas that year, and she told me someone had brought money to her mom and dad for her, and she went to town and bought the boys Christmas. She never did know who did that for her. She was so thankful. I believe that I was the only one who donated to her, which was just fine."

***

The doing of good deeds is important. As a free person, you can choose to live your life as a good person or as a bad person. To be a good person, do good deeds. To be a bad person, do bad deeds. If you do good deeds, you will become good. If you do bad deeds, you will become bad. To become the person you want to be, act as if you already are that kind of person. Each of us chooses what kind of person we will become. To become a good person, do the things a good person does. To become a bad person, do the things a bad person does. The opportunity to take action to become the kind of person you want to be is yours.

Educate Yourself
Read Like A Wolf Eats
Be Excellent to Each Other
Books Then, Books Now, Books Forever

***

In this retelling, as in all my retellings, I have tried to make the work of literature accessible to modern readers who may lack the knowledge about mythology, religion, and history that the literary work's contemporary audience had.

Do you know a language other than English? If you do, I give you permission to translate this book, copyright your translation, publish or self-publish it, and keep all the royalties for yourself. (Do give me credit, of course, for the original retelling.)

I would like to see my retellings of classic literature used in schools, so I give permission to the country of Finland (and all other countries) to give copies of this book to all students forever. I also give permission to the state of Texas (and all other states) to give copies of this book to all students forever. I also give permission to all teachers to give copies of this book to all students forever.

Teachers need not actually teach my retellings. Teachers are welcome to give students copies of my eBooks as background material. For example, if they are teaching Homer's *Iliad* and *Odyssey*, teachers are welcome to give students copies of my *Virgil's* Aeneid: *A Retelling in Prose* and tell students, "Here's another ancient epic you may want to read in your spare time."

CAST OF CHARACTERS

House of York

King Edward IV. King Edward IV and his wife, Queen Elizabeth, have two young sons, who are often referred to as the Princes:

Edward, Prince of Wales, and afterwards King Edward V; son of King Edward IV.

Richard, Duke of York; son of King Edward IV.

George, Duke of Clarence. Brother of King Edward IV. Clarence is the second-oldest brother.

Richard, Duke of Gloucester, and afterwards King Richard III. Brother of King Edward IV. Gloucester is the youngest brother.

Duchess of York. Mother of King Edward IV; George, Duke of Clarence; and Richard, Duke of Gloucester, who becomes King Richard III.

A young son of Clarence.

A young daughter of Clarence, named Margaret.

House of Lancaster

Queen Margaret. Widow of King Henry VI.

Lady Anne Neville. Widow of Edward, Prince of Wales (son of King Henry VI). She afterwards marries Richard.

Tressel and Berkeley, gentlemen attending on the Lady Anne.

Woodville Family

Queen Elizabeth, Queen of King Edward IV. Her maiden name was Elizabeth Woodville. Also called Lady Grey because she was the widow of Sir John Grey when King Edward IV married her. Among her children is young Elizabeth of York, who after the events of *Richard III* marries King Henry VII and becomes Queen Elizabeth. Neither Queen Elizabeth should be confused with Queen Elizabeth I. Two other children Queen Elizabeth had with her husband, King Edward IV, are Edward, Prince of Wales, and Richard, the young Duke of York.

Anthony Woodville, Earl Rivers. Brother of Queen Elizabeth, aka Lady Grey.

Marquess of Dorset. Son of Queen Elizabeth, aka Lady Grey. This son was from a marriage previous to that with King Edward IV. Dorset's father was Sir John Grey. A Marquess ranks above an Earl and below a Duke.

Lord Richard Grey. Son of Queen Elizabeth, aka Lady Grey. This son was from a marriage previous to that with King Edward IV. Grey's father was Sir John Grey.

Sir Thomas Vaughan. Ally of Earl Rivers and Lord Richard Grey.

King Richard III's Faction

Duke of Buckingham.

Sir William Catesby.

Duke of Norfolk.

Thomas Howard, Earl of Surrey. He is the Duke of Norfolk's son.

Sir Richard Ratcliff.

Sir James Tyrrel.

Lord Francis Lovel.

Earl of Richmond's Faction

Henry Tudor, Earl of Richmond, and afterwards King Henry VII.

Lord Stanley, Earl of Derby. Father of Earl of Richmond, who becomes King Henry VII.

Sir James Blunt.

Sir Walter Herbert.

Earl of Oxford.

Sir William Brandon.

Two Cardinals.

Clergy

Cardinal Bourchier, Archbishop of Canterbury.

Thomas Rotherham, Archbishop of York.

John Morton, Archbishop of Ely.

Christopher Urswick, a priest.

Second priest.

Other Characters

Lord William Hastings. He was Lord Chamberlain under King Edward IV.

Sir Robert Brakenbury. He was the Lieutenant of the Tower of London.

Lord Mayor of London.

Ghosts of those murdered by Richard III; Lords and other Attendants; a Pursuivant (a royal or state messenger who had the power to execute warrants), Scrivener, Citizens, Murderers, Messengers, Soldiers, Sheriff of Whitshire, etc.

Scene

England.

Note

See "Appendix A: Brief Historical Background" if you need a refresher on English history.

King Richard III reigned from 26 June 1483 to 22 August 1485.

CHAPTER 1

— 1.1 —

Richard, Duke of Gloucester, stood alone on a street in London near the Tower of London.

He said to himself, "Now is the winter of our discontent made glorious summer by this Sun of York."

For most people, this would be good news; the time of dissatisfaction was over. England had suffered from a long-lasting power struggle between the House of York and the House of Lancaster. This power struggle had ended with the Battle of Tewksbury in 1471 in which the Yorkists won a decisive victory over the Lancastrians. This had made secure the power of King Edward IV, a Yorkist. England was now at peace, but enmity still existed between the two Houses, aka families.

However, Richard, Duke of Gloucester, wanted to become King. Edward IV was his eldest brother, and George, Duke of Clarence, was the middle brother between King Edward IV and Richard, Duke of Gloucester. Richard would have to get rid of these two brothers if he were to become King.

When Richard, Duke of Gloucester, referred to "this Sun of York," he meant King Edward IV, whose emblem was a Sun.

Richard continued, "And all the clouds that scowled upon our House of York are buried in the deep bosom of the ocean. Our enemies have been conquered. Now our brows are bound with victorious wreaths. Our battered armor is hung up to serve as memorials. Our stern alarums — calls to arms — have been changed to merry meetings, and our dreadful martial marches to delightful measures of dance. Grim-faced war has smoothed his wrinkled forehead, and now, instead of mounting armored steeds to frighten the souls of fearful adversaries, he capers nimbly in a lady's chamber to the lascivious pleasing of a lute."

Instead of making war, people were now able to dance and to make love. To caper nimbly in a lady's chamber has a double meaning: It can mean to dance nimbly in a lady's room, or to 'dance' nimbly in a lady's vagina. A lute can be thought of as a phallic symbol.

Richard continued, "But I am not shaped for sexual sports, nor made to court an amorous, loving mirror."

Richard had been born prematurely, and he was physically handicapped. He walked with a limp, his arm was withered, and his back was hunched.

Richard continued, "I am rudely stamped and badly made, and lack love's majesty and so cannot strut before a wanton ambling nymph. I lack a fair bodily shape, and dissembling nature has cheated me by not giving me pleasing facial features. I am deformed, unfinished, sent before my time into this breathing, living world, scarcely half finished. I am so lame and so badly fashioned that dogs bark at me as I limp by them.

"Why, in this weak piping time of peace in which are heard the pipes of peace and not the fifes and drums of war, I have no delight to pass away the time, unless I delight to spy my shadow in the Sun and talk about my own deformity.

"And therefore, since I cannot show myself to be a lover, to while away these fair courteous and refined days, I am determined to prove that I am a villain and hate the frivolous and wanton pleasures of these days.

"I have lain plots and made dangerous first steps, using prophecies made under the influence of drunkenness, libels, and dreams to set my brothers George, who is the Duke of Clarence, and King Edward IV in deadly hate the one against the other.

"And if King Edward is as true and just as I am subtle, false, and treacherous, this day George, Duke of Clarence, should closely be confined and imprisoned because of a prophecy, which says that G shall murder King Edward IV's heirs."

King Edward IV thought that the G of the prophecy referred to George, Duke of Clarence. He should have thought that it referred to Richard, Duke of Gloucester.

Richard continued, "Dive, thoughts, down to my soul. I see Clarence coming toward me."

George, Duke of Clarence, was being guarded. With him was Sir Robert Brakenbury, Lieutenant of the Tower of London.

Richard said to Clarence, "Brother, good day. What is the meaning of this armed guard who waits upon your grace?"

Clarence joked, "His majesty, King Edward IV, my brother, being concerned about my personal safety, has appointed this guard to convey me to the Tower of London."

Clarence knew that he was under arrest on a serious charge, but he was able to joke. King Edward IV was his brother, and he felt that eventually they would be reconciled.

Richard asked, "Upon what cause are they taking you to the Tower of London?"

"The cause is that my name is George: George, Duke of Clarence."

"Alas, my lord, that fault is none of yours," Richard said. "Edward IV should, to punish that fault, commit your godfathers to the Tower. Your godfathers were present at your baptism and naming. Perhaps his majesty has some intention that you shall be newly christened and renamed in the Tower. But what's the matter, Clarence? May I know? Can you tell me?"

"Yes, Richard, when I know," Clarence replied, "for I protest that as of now I do not know why King Edward IV is imprisoning me, but as far as I can learn, he is paying attention to prophecies and dreams, and from the alphabet he plucks the letter G, and says that a wizard told him that G would disinherit his children and prevent them from ever succeeding to the throne. And, because my name George begins with G, he thinks that I am the G of the prophecy. These things, as far as I can learn, and other trifles such as these have moved his highness to imprison me now in the Tower."

"Why, this is what happens when men are ruled by women," Richard replied. "It is not the King who sends you to the Tower. Clarence, Lady Grey — the King's wife — is the woman who has persuaded him to do this extreme action."

Richard used the less complimentary title Lady Grey instead of her proper title: Queen Elizabeth, wife of Edward IV. She was the widow of Sir John Grey when King Edward IV married her.

Richard continued, "Was it not she and that good man of worship, Anthony Woodville, her brother there, who made Edward IV send Lord William Hastings to the Tower, from whence today he is delivered?"

Again, Richard was using a less-complimentary term. Anthony Woodville was the Earl Rivers. Richard was using his family name, not his title of Earl.

Also, a goodman was a man of substance, but not a man of gentle — noble — birth.

Richard continued, "We are not safe, Clarence; we are not safe."

Clarence replied, "By Heaven, I think there's no man who is secure except the Queen's relatives and the night-walking heralds who trudge between the King and Mistress Shore."

A night-walker is a criminal, but here the heralds — actually, messengers — walk at night because they are engaged on a mission that they need to keep secret. They are arranging assignations between King Edward IV and his mistress, Mistress Jane Shore, a commoner. Mistress is a title that means Ms. or Mrs.

Clarence continued, "Haven't you heard what a humble suppliant Lord Hastings was to Mistress Shore for his delivery from the Tower?"

"Humbly complaining to her deity got the Lord Chamberlain — Hastings — his liberty," Richard said. "I'll tell you what; I think it is our best course of action, if we want to keep in the King's favor, to be her men and wear her livery."

Again, Richard was belittling his enemies. Jane Shore was a commoner, and so her servants did not wear her livery — distinctive uniforms that would identify them as being employed by her.

Richard continued, "The jealous over-worn widow and herself, since our brother the King dubbed them gentlewomen, are mighty gossips in this monarchy."

The "jealous over-worn widow" was Queen Elizabeth, widow of Sir John Grey, and understandably jealous of Mistress Shore. Richard was calling both Queen Elizabeth and Mistress Shore chatterers who had a lot of power because of their relationships to King Edward IV. Richard was again mocking the Queen; she had been born a gentlewoman, so her new husband had not made her a gentlewoman. Mistress Shore, of course, was a commoner.

Brakenbury had allowed the two men to talk because of Richard's high rank as Duke of Gloucester, but now he intervened to enforce King Edward IV's orders. Brakenbury did not want to make an enemy of Richard, but he also did not want to make an enemy of Edward IV.

Brakenbury said, "I beseech your graces both to pardon me, but his majesty has strictly ordered that no man — no matter how high his rank — shall have private conversation with Clarence, his brother."

Richard replied, "So be it. If it please your worship, Brakenbury, you may listen to anything we say."

Richard again was being mocking. He had called Brakenbury "your worship," as if Brakenbury had a higher rank than his. Richard was a Duke, while Brakenbury was only a knight.

Richard continued, "We speak no treason, man. We say the King is wise and virtuous, and his noble Queen is well struck in years, fair, and not jealous. We say that Shore's wife has a pretty foot, a cherry lip, a bonny eye, and a surpassingly pleasing tongue, and we say that the Queen's relatives are made gentlefolks. What do you say, sir? Can you deny all this?"

"My lord, I myself have nought to do with this," Brakenbury replied.

"Naught to do with Mistress Shore!" Richard said. "I tell you, fellow, he who does naught with her, excepting one, should realize that it is best he do it secretly and without witnesses."

Richard had changed Brakenbury's "nought" to "naught." "Nought" means "nothing," but "naught" means "naughtiness or sex."

"Which one, my lord?"

"Her husband, knave," Richard said. "Would you betray me?"

Richard, of course, was alluding to Edward IV's affair with Mistress Shore. It was best that such an affair be carried on by the principals secretly, and it was best for other people to not speak about it.

"I beseech your grace to pardon me, and at the same time I ask you to cease your conversation with the noble Duke of Clarence."

Clarence said, "We know your orders, Brakenbury, and we will obey."

"We are the Queen's abject subjects, and we must obey," Richard said, again making the point that Edward IV was being controlled by women — especially Queen Elizabeth.

Richard said to Clarence, "Brother, farewell. I will go to the King, and whatsoever you want me to do, even if it is to call King Edward's widow 'sister,' I will perform it to free you."

King Edward's widow was the still-living Queen Elizabeth — she was the widow he had married: Lady Grey. Richard was saying it would be hard for him to be civil to her and call her his sister-in-law, but he was willing to do that if it would make Clarence a free man.

Richard added, "In the meantime, this deep disgrace in brotherhood touches me deeper than you can imagine."

The "deep disgrace in brotherhood" referred to two disgraces: 1) Edward IV's imprisonment of his brother Clarence, and 2) Richard's plotting against his two brothers: Edward IV and the Duke of Clarence.

In addition, "touches me deeper than you can imagine" had two meanings: 1) distresses me more than you can imagine, and 2) concerns me — and my deep plot to make myself King — more than you can imagine.

Richard was capable of crocodile tears. Weeping, he hugged his brother.

"I know it pleases neither of us well," Clarence said.

"Well, your imprisonment shall not be long. In the meantime, have patience."

"I must, necessarily. Farewell."

Clarence, Brakenbury, and the guard departed to go to the Tower of London.

Richard said to himself, "Go, tread the path from which you shall never return. Simple, plain Clarence! I love you so much that I will shortly send your soul to Heaven, if Heaven will take the present from my hands. But who is coming toward me? The newly freed Hastings!"

Hastings walked over to Richard and said, "Good time of day to my gracious lord!"

"As much to my good Lord Chamberlain!" Richard said. "You are very welcome to the open air. How has your lordship endured your imprisonment?"

"With patience, noble lord, as prisoners must," Hastings replied, "but I shall live, my lord, to give 'thanks' to those who were the cause of my imprisonment."

"No doubt, no doubt; and so shall Clarence, too, for those who were your enemies are also his, and they have prevailed as much over him as over you."

"It is all the more pity that the eagle should be mewed, while kites and buzzards prey at liberty."

The eagle, a noble bird, was Clarence, a nobleman. He was mewed — imprisoned — while the lesser birds of prey who were his enemies — kites and buzzards — were still free to wreak harm on others.

"What is the news abroad?" Richard asked.

Hastings was able to joke despite his imprisonment. By "abroad," Richard had meant "current, being discussed now." Hastings deliberately misinterpreted it as meaning "in other countries," but he still gave Richard the information he wanted.

"No news is so bad abroad as this news we have at home. The King is sickly, weak, and melancholy, and his physicians fear mightily that he will die."

"Now, by Saint Paul, this news is bad indeed," Richard said. "Oh, he has kept an evil way of life for a long time, and he has excessively consumed and wasted his royal person. This is very grievous to think about. What, is he in his bed?"

"He is."

"Go ahead of me to the court, and I will follow you."

Hastings departed.

Richard said to himself, "He cannot live, I hope, and he must not die until George, Duke of Clarence, be galloped as quickly as possible up to Heaven. I'll go in and see him so I can urge him even more to hate Clarence. I will use lies well steeled with weighty arguments. And, if my deep plot does not fail, Clarence has not another day left in which to live. Once Clarence is dead, then I hope that God takes King Edward IV into his mercy and leaves the world for me to bustle in!

"For then I'll marry the Earl of Warwick's youngest daughter: Lady Anne Neville. She is the widow of Edward, Prince of Wales, who was the son of King Henry VI.

"What though I killed her husband and her father-in-law? The readiest way to make the wench amends is to become her husband and her father. This I will do, not so much for love as for another secret purpose for which I must marry her — if I marry her, I can make more secure my future crown as King Richard III of England. But I am running before my horse to market — I am running ahead of myself because I am not yet King. Clarence still breathes; Edward still lives and reigns. When they are gone, that is the time for me to count my gains."

On another street in London, the corpse of King Henry VI lay in an open coffin on a bier. Four gentlemen carried the bier. Attendants carrying halberds — a combined spear and battle-ax — guarded the body. Mourning the body was Lady Anne, King Henry VI's daughter-in-law. Only nine or so people were present, including the gentlemen who were carrying the bier. Two of Lady Anne's attendants, Tressel and Berkeley, were with her. The ruling party wanted little attention given to the disposal of King Henry VI's corpse, and Lady Anne was being defiant by publicly mourning his death.

Lady Anne said, "Set down your honorable load, if honor may be shrouded in a coffin — does honor belong only to the living? Wait while I for a while lament as a mourner with proper regard for the untimely fall of virtuous Lancaster. The fall of the Lancastrian King Henry VI is also the fall of the House of Lancaster! Poor figure of a holy King! Your body is as cold as an iron key during winter. Pale remains of the House of Lancaster! You bloodless remnant of that royal blood! May it be lawful that I call upon your ghost, as if you were a saint, to hear the lamentations of Poor Anne, who was wife to your Edward, your slaughtered son, stabbed by the selfsame hand — that of Richard, Duke of Gloucester — that made these wounds that killed you! In these windows — your wounds — that let forth your life, I pour the unavailing and useless balm of my poor eyes — my tears.

"Cursed be the hand that made these fatal holes in your body! Cursed be the heart that had the heart to do it! Cursed be the blood that let this blood flow from out of your body! May a more direful fortune befall that hated wretch, who makes us wretched by your death, than I can wish to adders, spiders, toads, or any creeping poisonous thing that lives!

"If your murderer should ever have a child, let it be defective, monstrous, and prematurely brought to light. Let it have an ugly and unnatural appearance that will frighten the hopeful mother when she looks at it, and let that child be the heir to his evil, wrongdoing, and unhappiness!

"If he should ever have a wife, let her be made as miserable by the death of him as I am made by the deaths of my poor husband and you! Let her suffer from the death of a loved one as I have suffered!"

She said to the pallbearers, "Come, now let us go towards the monastery of Chertsey near London with your holy load, which we have taken from Saint Paul's Cathedral to be interred there, and whenever you are weary from carrying the weight, rest yourselves while I lament King Henry VI's corpse."

The pallbearers lifted the bier.

Richard, Duke of Gloucester, walked up to the group of people and said, "Stop, you who bear the corpse, and set it down."

Lady Anne said, "What black magician has conjured up this fiend to stop our holy and charitable deeds?"

"Villains, set down the corpse," Richard said, "or, by Saint Paul, I'll make a corpse of him who disobeys me."

A gentleman said, "My lord, stand back, and let the coffin pass."

"Unmannered dog!" Richard said. "Halt, when I command you to. Stop pointing your halberd at my chest and instead hold it upright, or, by Saint Paul, I'll strike you with my foot and spurn you, beggar, for your boldness in disobeying me."

The pallbearers set down the bier.

Lady Anne said to them, "Do you tremble? Are you all afraid? I don't blame you, for you are mortal, and mortal eyes cannot endure the devil."

She said to Richard, "Avaunt, you dreadful minister of Hell!"

The word "avaunt" was a strong way of saying "get lost" and was used in addressing malevolent spirits.

She continued, "You had power only over the mortal body of King Henry VI. His soul you have no power over and cannot have; therefore, be gone."

Richard replied, "Sweet saint, for charity, be not so curst and ill-tempered."

Lady Anne said to Richard, "Foul devil, for God's sake, go away from here and stop troubling us, for you have made the happy Earth your Hell. You have filled it with cursing cries and deep outcries. If you delight to view your heinous deeds, behold this corpse — this example of your butcheries."

She said to the men with her, "Gentlemen, see, see! The dead King Henry VI's wounds open their congealed mouths and bleed afresh! Such things happen when a corpse is in the presence of its murderer!"

She said to Richard, "Blush, blush, you lump of foul deformity, for it is your presence that draws out this blood from cold and empty veins where no blood dwells. Your murderous deed, which is inhuman and unnatural, provokes this most unnatural deluge of blood.

"God, Who made King Henry VI's blood, revenge his death!

"Earth, which drinks King Henry VI's blood, revenge his death!

"May either Heaven with lightning strike the murderer dead or Earth gape wide open and eat Richard quickly, as quickly as you swallow up this good King Henry VI's blood that Richard's Hell-governed arm has butchered!"

Richard replied, "Lady, you know no rules of Christian charity, which renders good for bad, and blessings for curses."

"Villain, you know no law of God or man," Lady Anne said. "No beast is so fierce but that it knows some touch of pity."

"But I know none, and I therefore am no beast."

"You are not a beast, and you are not a man. It's wonderful when devils tell the truth!"

"It is more to be wondered at when angels are so angry," Richard said. "Grant me, you divine perfection of a woman, the opportunity to acquit myself in detail of these supposed evils."

"Grant me, you shapeless plague of a man, the opportunity to curse your cursed self in detail for these known evils."

"You who are more beautiful than tongue can say, let me have some patient leisure time in which to explain to you my actions."

"You who are fouler than any heart can think you to be, you can make no justified excuse for your actions other than to hang yourself."

"By such despair, I should accuse myself," Richard said.

Lady Anne said, "Yes, and also, by despairing, you should stand excused for your sin because you would do worthy vengeance on yourself, who did unworthy and undeserved slaughter upon others."

The despair they meant was the kind that involved believing that Richard had sinned so greatly that God was incapable of forgiving him. That kind of despair meant committing the sin of pride since God is merciful and can forgive any sin that is sincerely repented. That kind of despair also often results in committing suicide, which is another sin. Dante's *Inferno* describes a ring in Hell that includes the suicides. Lady Anne would be happy if Richard were to despair, commit suicide, and be damned to Hell for eternity.

Richard said, "Suppose that I did not kill your husband and your father-in-law: Prince Edward and King Henry VI."

"Why, then they would not be dead, but they are dead, and you devilish slave, you murdered them."

"I did not kill your husband."

"Why, then he is alive."

"No, he is dead; King Edward IV's hand slew him."

"In your foul throat you lie," Lady Anne said. "Queen Margaret, the wife of King Henry VI, saw your murderous sword steaming with his blood. That same sword you once pointed at her breast and would have used to murder her if your brothers — Clarence and Edward IV — had not beaten aside the swordpoint."

"I was provoked by Queen Margaret's slanderous tongue, which laid the guilt of my two brothers upon my guiltless shoulders."

"You were provoked by your own bloody mind, which never dreamt about anything but butcheries," Lady Anne said. "Did you not kill this King — Henry VI?"

"I grant you that I did," Richard said.

"You grant me, hedgehog?" Lady Anne said, mockingly referring to Richard's emblem, which was a boar.

An emblem is a heraldic device that symbolizes a family or person.

She continued, "Then, may God grant me something, too — that you be damned for that wicked deed! Oh, King Henry VI was gentle, mild, and virtuous!"

"Then he was all the fitter for the King of Heaven, Who has him."

"He is in Heaven, where you shall never come."

"Let King Henry VI thank me, who helped to send him to Heaven, for he was fitter for that place than Earth."

"And you are unfit for any place but Hell."

"I am fit for one other place, if you will hear me name it," Richard said.

"You are fit for some dungeon."

"I am fit for your bedchamber."

"May troubled sleep be the rule in any bedchamber where you lie!"

"That will be the case, madam, until I lie with you."

"I hope so," Lady Anne said. "You will never lie with me, and so you will always endure troubled sleep."

"I know so," Richard said. "I know that I will endure troubled sleep until I lie with you. But, gentle Lady Anne, let us leave this keen encounter of our wits, and fall somewhat into a slower method of thinking. Isn't the causer of the untimely deaths of these Plantagenets, King Henry VI and his only son, Prince Edward, as blameful as the executioner?"

"You are the cause, and you are the most accursed effect," Lady Anne replied.

The word "effect" usually means "result," but Lady Anne was using it in the sense of "fulfillment." She meant that Richard was fully responsible for the two murders — he had been the cause of the fulfillment — accomplishment — of the two murders.

In his reply, Richard used the word "effect" with its usual meaning of "result": "Your beauty was the cause of that effect. Your beauty that haunted me in my sleep caused me to undertake the death of all of the world, so that I might live one hour in your sweet bosom. Your beauty caused me to act as I did."

"If I thought that, I tell you, murderer, my fingernails should rend that beauty from my cheeks."

"These eyes could never endure sweet beauty's destruction," Richard replied. "You would not blemish your beauty, if I stood by — I would stop you. As all the world is cheered by the Sun, so I am cheered by your beauty; your beauty is my day, my life."

"May black night darken your day, and may death darken your life!"

"Curse not yourself, fair creature — you are both my day and my life."

"I wish I were, so I could be revenged on you," Lady Anne said. "I would end that day and that life."

"It is a most unnatural quarrel to be revenged on the man who loves you."

"It is a quarrel just and reasonable to be revenged on him who slew my husband."

"He who bereft you, lady, of your husband, did it to help you to a better husband."

"His better does not breathe upon the earth."

"He lives who loves you better than he — Prince Edward — could."

"Name him."

"Plantagenet," Richard replied.

Richard, Duke of Gloucester, was a Plantagenet, by virtue of being a York; however, Prince Edward, Lady Anne's late husband, was also a Plantagenet, by virtue of being a Lancaster. The House of York and the House of Lancaster shared a common ancestry. One of the sons of King Edward III — who was a Plantagenet — was John of Gaunt, first Duke of Lancaster. Another of King Edward III's sons was Edmund of Langley, first Duke of York.

"Why, Prince Edward was a Plantagenet," Lady Anne replied.

"I mean a person with the same name, but with a better nature."

"Where is he?"

"Here he is. I am he."

Lady Anne spit at him. According to folklore, this was a way to ward off the malevolent influence of the evil eye.

Richard asked, "Why do you spit at me?"

"I wish it were deadly poison, for your sake!" Lady Anne replied.

"Poison has never come from so sweet a place."

"Never has poison hung on a fouler toad than you! Get out of my sight! You infect my eyes."

"Your eyes, sweet lady, have infected mine."

In this culture, one person's eyes were thought to be able to affect another person's eyes. For example, people thought that illness could be transferred through glances from sore eyes. However, people also believed that love entered the body through the eyes.

"I wish that my eyes were basilisks, to strike you dead!"

Basilisks were mythological creatures that could kill simply by looking at a living thing.

"I wish they were, that I might die at once, immediately and once and for all, for now they kill me with a living death," Richard said. "Your eyes have from mine drawn salt tears. Your eyes have caused me to shame the appearance of my eyes with a store of childish drops — tears. Your eyes have done that to these eyes of mine that have never before shed a remorseful tear.

"No, I did not weep even when my father — Richard Plantagenet, Duke of York — and my brother Edward, who is now King, wept when they heard the piteous moan that my late brother Edmund, Earl of Rutland, made when the black-faced and darkly angry Lancastrian supporter John de Clifford shook his sword at him and then killed him. No, I did not weep even when your warlike father, the Earl of Warwick, like a child, told the sad story of my father's death and paused twenty times to sob and weep. All the bystanders who heard your father tell the tale wet their cheeks like trees dashed with rain, but in that sad time my manly eyes scorned to shed even one humble tear.

"But what these sorrows could not do — make me cry — your beauty has. Your beauty has made my eyes blind with weeping. I never sued to friend or enemy. My tongue could never learn sweet, smooth, flattering words. But now your beauty is proposed my fee, and so my proud heart sues, and prompts my tongue to speak. If speaking and pleading will earn for me your beauty, then I will speak and plead."

Lady Anne looked scornfully at Richard.

Richard said, "Teach not your lips such scorn, for they were made for kissing, lady, not for such contempt. If your revengeful heart cannot forgive me, then here and now I give you this sharp-pointed sword, which if you please to hide it in my true and faithful bosom and let the soul that adores you leave my body, I lay it naked to the deadly stroke, and humbly beg the death that follows judgment upon my knee."

Richard gave her his sword, knelt, and opened his shirt to lay bare his chest. Lady Anne pointed the sword at his chest, and then she paused.

Richard said, "No, do not pause, for I did kill King Henry VI, but it was your beauty that provoked me to kill him. Now dispatch me; it was I who stabbed young Prince Edward, your husband, but it was your Heavenly face that set me on."

Lady Anne dropped the sword.

Richard said, "Take up the sword again, or take up me."

Richard was in the position of a suppliant. If Lady Anne were to take his hand and help him up, she would be accepting his suit by showing mercy to the suppliant.

She said, "Arise, dissembler. Although I wish your death, I will not be the executioner."

Richard rose, unassisted, and said, "Then order me to kill myself, and I will do it."

"I have already done that."

"Tush, you said that in your rage. and even with the word, that hand which for your love did kill your love — your husband — shall, for your love, kill a far truer love — mine. To both their deaths you shall be an accessary."

"I wish that I knew what was in your heart."

"What is in my heart appears in my tongue — with the words I say, I express what is in my heart."

"I am afraid that both your heart and your tongue are false and treacherous."

"Then no man has ever been true and faithful."

"Well, well, sheathe your sword," Lady Anne said.

"Say, then, my peace is made," Richard said. "Say that we have made peace between us."

The terms that Richard wanted with the peace treaty included marriage to Lady Anne.

"That you shall know hereafter."

"But shall I live in hope?"

"All men, I hope, live in hope."

"Agree to wear this ring," Richard said, holding out a ring.

"To take is not to give," Lady Anne replied.

Richard put the ring on Lady Anne's finger and said, "Just like this ring encompasses your finger, even so your breast encloses my poor heart. Wear both of them, for both of them are yours. And if your poor devoted suppliant may but beg one favor at your gracious hand, you will confirm his happiness forever."

"What favor do you wish?"

"That it would please you to leave these sad designs — the funeral arrangement for King Henry VI — to a man who has more cause to be a mourner. I want you to immediately go to Crosby Place, one of my residences in London, where, after I have solemnly interred at Chertsey monastery this noble King, and wet his grave with my repentant tears, I will with all speedy and expeditious duty see you. For many secret reasons, I beg you, grant me this favor."

"With all my heart, I grant it, and it gives me much joy, too, to see you have become so penitent."

She ordered her attendants, "Tressel and Berkeley, go along with me."

"Tell me farewell," Richard said.

"Faring well is more than you deserve," Lady Anne replied, "but since you are teaching me how to flatter you, imagine I have said farewell already."

Lady Anne, Tressel, and Berkeley departed.

"Sirs, take up the corpse," Richard said to the pallbearers.

"Towards Chertsey, noble lord?" one of the pallbearers asked.

"No, to Whitefriars; there await my coming."

Whitefriars was a monastery in London. Richard had no real reason to have the corpse taken there rather than to Chertsey, except to be contrary and not do what he had told Lady Anne he would do.

Everyone departed, leaving Richard by himself.

Pleased with how his courtship of Lady Anne had gone, he said to himself, "Was ever a woman in this manner wooed? Was ever a woman in this manner won? I'll have her, legally and sexually, but I will not keep her long.

"What! I, who killed her husband, Prince Edward, and his father, King Henry VI, have taken and conquered Lady Anne when her heart was filled with the extremest hate of me, when she had curses for me in her mouth and tears in her eyes, when the bleeding witness — the corpse of King Henry VI — of her hatred for me was nearby, when God, her conscience, and these obstructions were all against me, and I had nothing to back my wooing of her at all except the plain devil and dissembling, hypocritical looks, and yet I won her, with all the world against me and nothing for me! Ha!

"Has she already forgotten that brave Prince Edward, her lord and husband, whom I, some three months ago, stabbed in my angry mood in the Battle of Tewksbury? A sweeter and a lovelier gentleman, created with the prodigality and generosity of nature, young, valiant, wise, and, no doubt, extremely royal and made to be a King, the spacious world cannot again afford, and will she yet debase and lower her eyes on me, who cropped the golden prime of this sweet Prince, and made her widow to a woeful bed? She will lower her eyes on me, whose all does not equal Prince Edward's half? On me, who limps and is misshapen?

"I bet my Dukedom against a beggarly small coin that I have been mistaken about my personal appearance all this while. Upon my life, she finds, although I cannot, that I am a marvelously handsome man. I'll buy a mirror, and pay some score or two of tailors to study fashions to adorn my body. Since I am crept in favor with myself, and have discovered that I am handsome, I will maintain my appearance with some little cost.

"But first I'll dump yonder fellow into his grave, and then I will return lamenting to my 'love': Lady Anne.

"Shine out, fair Sun, until I have bought a mirror, so that I may see my shadow as I walk."

In a room of the palace was Queen Elizabeth, wife of the very ill King Edward IV. With her were Rivers, Dorset, and Grey.

Queen Elizabeth's maiden name was Elizabeth Woodville.

Rivers was Anthony Woodville, Earl Rivers, and he was the brother of Queen Elizabeth.

Dorset was the Marquess of Dorset, and he was a son of Queen Elizabeth, aka Lady Grey. This son was from a marriage previous to that with King Edward IV. Dorset's father was Sir John Grey.

Grey, Dorset's brother, was Lord Richard Grey, another son of Queen Elizabeth. This son was from a marriage previous to that with King Edward IV. Grey's father was Sir John Grey.

Rivers said to his sister, Queen Elizabeth, "Have patience, madam. There's no doubt that his majesty will soon recover his accustomed health."

Queen Elizabeth's son Grey said to her, "When you badly endure his illness, it makes him worse. Therefore, for God's sake, allow yourself to be comforted, and cheer up his grace with quick and merry words."

"If my husband the King were dead, what would happen to me?" Queen Elizabeth asked.

"No other harm but loss of such a lord and husband," Rivers, her brother, replied.

"The loss of such a lord and husband includes all harm," she said.

Grey said, "The Heavens have blessed you with a goodly son to be your comforter when he is gone."

That son was the young Edward, the current Prince of Wales.

"Oh, he is young and while he is too young to govern, his power will be put unto the trust of Richard, Duke of Gloucester, a man who does not love me, or any of you. If my son Edward becomes King of England, then because Edward is so young, Richard will have the royal power until Edward becomes an adult."

"Is it concluded that Richard shall be Lord Protector?" Rivers asked.

"It has been decided that he will be, but the decision is not officially made yet, but it will be officially made, if King Edward IV dies," Queen Elizabeth said.

The Duke of Buckingham and Lord Stanley, who was the Earl of Derby, entered the room.

Grey said, "Here come the lords of Buckingham and Derby."

Buckingham greeted Queen Elizabeth, "Good time of day unto your royal grace!"

Lord Stanley greeted Queen Elizabeth, "May God make your majesty as joyful as you have been!"

Queen Elizabeth replied, "The Countess Richmond, my good Lord Stanley, to your good prayers will scarcely say amen."

The Countess Richmond was Lord Stanley's wife. Her maiden name was Margaret Beaufort, and her first marriage was to Edmund Tudor, first Earl of Richmond, with whom she had had a son: Henry Tudor, second Earl of Richmond. Henry Tudor had inherited his father's title. One of Countess Richmond's ancestors was King Edward III. Henry Tudor was a member of the House of Lancaster.

Queen Elizabeth continued, "Still, Lord Stanley, notwithstanding she's your wife, and she does not love me, I want you, my good lord, to be assured that I do not hate you on account of her proud arrogance."

"I beg you," Lord Stanley said, "either to not believe the malicious slanders of her false accusers, or, if she is justly accused, to bear with her weakness, which I think proceeds from chronic sickness, and not from firmly grounded and deeply rooted malice."

Rivers asked, "Did you see the King today, Lord Stanley?"

"Just now the Duke of Buckingham and I have come from visiting his majesty."

"What is the likelihood of his recovery from his illness, lords?" Queen Elizabeth asked.

"Madam, there is good hope of recovery," Buckingham replied. "His grace speaks cheerfully."

"May God grant him health!" Queen Elizabeth said. "Did you talk with him?"

"Madam, we did," Buckingham said. "He desires to make reconciliation between the Duke of Gloucester and your brothers, and between them and Hastings, who is the Lord Chamberlain, and he sent people to summon them to his royal presence."

"I wish that all were well!" Queen Elizabeth said. "But that will never be. I fear that our happiness is at the highest point and will soon suffer a decline."

Richard, Duke of Gloucester, and Lord Chamberlain Hastings entered the room.

Pretending to be angry, Richard complained, "They do me wrong, and I will not endure it! Who are they who complain to King Edward IV that I indeed am stern and do not love and respect them?

"By holy Saint Paul, they love his grace only lightly when they fill his ears with such dissentious rumors. Because I cannot flatter and speak nicely, smile in men's faces, smooth and conciliate, deceive and cheat, duck with French nods in ostentatious bows and apish courtesy, I must be held to be a rancorous enemy.

"Cannot a plain man live and think no harm, but his simple truth must be abused like this by silken, sly, insinuating Jacks?"

Jacks are lowly born fellows.

Rivers asked, "To whom present here is your grace speaking?"

"To you," Richard said, insultingly, "who has neither honesty nor grace. When have I injured you? When have I done you wrong? Or you, Dorset? Or you, Grey? Or any of your faction? A plague upon you all! His royal person the King — whom I hope God may preserve better than you would wish! — cannot be quiet scarcely the time it takes him to catch his breath, but you must trouble him with lewd complaints."

Queen Elizabeth said, "Brother-in-law Richard, Duke of Gloucester, you are mistaken about this matter. The King, of his own royal disposition, and not provoked by any suitor, thinking, probably, of your interior hatred, which in your outward actions shows itself against my kindred, brothers, and myself, has sent for you so that thereby he may learn the grounds of your ill will toward us, and so remove it."

"I don't know what to think," Richard said. "The world has grown so bad, that wrens make prey where eagles dare not perch. Since every Jack has become a gentleman, there's many a gentle, noble person made a Jack."

A Jack was an item used in the game of bowls. The Jack was a small bowl, or ball, that was targeted by larger bowls. Another meaning of "Jack" was "lowly born person."

Richard was complaining because when his brother, King Edward IV, had married Elizabeth and made her Queen, her family — the Woodvilles — had been elevated to a high social status. And he was saying that some highly born people — such as his brother Clarence and Lord Chamberlain Hastings — were being targeted by the newly elevated people.

Queen Elizabeth said, "Come, come, we know your meaning, brother-in-law Richard, Duke of Gloucester; you envy my advancement and my kinsmen's. May God grant we never may have need of you!"

"In the meantime, God grants that we have need of you," Richard replied. "Your brother-in-law, Clarence, who is my brother, is imprisoned by your means, I myself am disgraced, and the nobility is held in contempt, while many fair promotions are daily given to ennoble those who scarcely, even two days ago, were worth a noble."

The word "noble" referred both to a coin called a noble and to a nobleman or noblewoman. Richard, as Queen Elizabeth realized, was complaining about her family's great rise in status and many promotions as a result of her marriage to Edward IV.

She replied, "By Him — God — Who raised me to this filled-with-worries height from that contented fortune that I previously enjoyed, I have never incensed his majesty the King against the Duke of Clarence, but I have instead been an earnest advocate to plead for him. My lord, you do me shameful injury when you falsely draw me into these vile suspicions."

"You may deny that you were not the cause of my Lord Hastings' recent imprisonment," Richard replied.

Rivers said, "She may, my lord, for —"

Richard interrupted, "She may, Lord Rivers! Why, who does not knows that? She may do more, sir, than deny that. She may help you to many fair promotions, and then deny her aiding hand therein, and instead say that your 'great merit' deserved those honors. What may she not? She may, yes, marry, may she —"

"What, marry, may she?" Rivers asked.

The word "marry," as used by Rivers, was a mild oath, meaning "By the Virgin Mary."

"What, marry, may she!" Richard said. "Marry with a King, a bachelor, a handsome stripling, too. Certainly your grandmother had a worse match."

Richard was making fun of Queen Elizabeth's age; she was older than her husband. And by saying that Rivers' grandmother had made a worse match, he meant that she had not married a King; indeed, Queen Elizabeth's family was far from belonging to the top aristocracy until she married the King.

Queen Elizabeth said, "My Lord of Gloucester, I have too long endured your blunt upbraidings and your bitter scoffs. By Heaven, I will acquaint his majesty with those gross taunts of yours that I have often endured. I had rather be a country servant-maid than a great Queen with this way of life, being thus taunted, scorned, and baited at."

The baiting she referred to was bear-baiting, in which bears were tied to a stake and tormented by dogs.

The old Queen Margaret entered the room in time to hear Queen Elizabeth say, "Small joy have I in being England's Queen."

The old Queen Margaret was the widow of King Henry VI. She was bitter about his death and the death of her son: Prince Edward.

She said to herself, "God, I pray that you lessen that small joy that she feels! Her honor, status, and throne are all my due. They belong to me, not to her."

Richard said to Queen Elizabeth, "What! You threaten me that you will tell the King what I am saying? Tell him, and leave out nothing. Everything that I have said I will avouch to be true in the presence of the King. I dare to risk being sent to the Tower of London in retaliation. It is time for me to speak up; my pains are quite forgotten."

Richard meant the pains that he had taken to make his brother Edward King of England, but the old Queen Margaret took "pains" to mean the pains that Richard had inflicted on her family.

She said to herself, "Damn, devil! I remember those pains all too well. You slew my husband, King Henry VI, in the Tower of London, and you slew Prince Edward, my poor son, in the Battle of Tewksbury."

Richard said to Queen Elizabeth, "Before you were Queen or your husband was King, I was a pack-horse — a toiler — in his great affairs. I was a weeder-out of his proud adversaries and a liberal rewarder of his friends. To make his blood royal, I spilt my own blood."

"Yes, and you spilt much better blood than your brother's or your own," the old Queen Margaret said to herself.

Richard continued, "In all which time you and your then-husband, Sir John Grey, were supporters of the House of Lancaster — and so were you, Rivers. Queen Elizabeth, wasn't your husband slain in old Queen Margaret's army in the Battle of Saint Albans? Let me put in your minds, if you have forgotten, what you have been before now, and what you are now, and in addition, what I have been, and what I am now."

"You have been a murderous villain, and you still are," the old Queen Margaret said to herself.

Richard said, "Poor Clarence did forsake his father-in-law, the Earl of Warwick; yes, he forswore and perjured himself — which may Jesus pardon!"

"Which may God revenge!" the old Queen Margaret said to herself.

George, Duke of Clarence, had married Isabella, one of the Earl of Warwick's daughters — Lady Anne was her sister — and for a while he had fought for the House of Lancaster. However, he changed sides and fought for the House of York and helped to make his brother Edward King of England.

Richard continued, "Clarence fought on Edward's side for the crown, and for his reward, poor lord, he is locked up in the Tower of London. I wish to God my heart were flint, like Edward's, or I wish that Edward's heart were soft and pitiful, like mine. I am too foolish — like a child — for this world."

"Hurry yourself to Hell for shame, and leave the world, you evil demon! There your kingdom is," the old Queen Margaret said to herself.

Rivers said to Richard, "My Lord of Gloucester, in those busy days that here you bring up to prove us enemies, we followed then our lord, our lawful King. Likewise, we would follow you, if you should ever be our King."

"If I should be!" Richard said. "I had rather be a peddler than be King. Far be from my heart the thought of being King!"

Queen Elizabeth said to Richard, "As little joy, my lord, as you suppose you should enjoy, were you this country's King, may you suppose me to enjoy as the Queen of this Kingdom."

The old Queen Margaret, who regarded herself as the rightful Queen of England, said to herself, "The Queen truly enjoys little joy, for I am the rightful Queen, and I am entirely joyless. I can no longer hold my tongue."

She advanced toward the others and said loudly to them, "Hear me, you wrangling pirates, who fall out with each other in sharing that which you have pillaged from me! Which of you who looks on me does not tremble? I am the rightful Queen, and if you don't bow to me like subjects, then — because you deposed me — you quake like rebels!"

Richard turned as if he were going to walk away, but the old Queen Margaret said to him, "Oh, gentle villain, do not turn away!"

"Gentle villain" was an insult. Richard was gentle — highly born — but he was also a villain.

Richard replied to her, "Foul wrinkled witch, what are you doing in my sight?"

Many people in England believed that witches existed.

Old Queen Margaret replied, "I am making an account of everything that you have marred and ruined. I will make that account before I let you go."

"Weren't you banished from England on pain of death?" Richard asked.

"I was, but I find more pain in banishment from England than death can give me if I make my abode here. Richard, you owe me a husband and a son. All of you here owe me a Kingdom, and all of you here owe me allegiance: The sorrows that I have by rights are yours, and all the pleasures that you usurp are mine."

Richard said, "My noble father laid a curse on you when you set on his warlike brows a paper crown and with your scorns drew rivers of tears from his eyes, and then, so he could dry his tears, you gave my father — the third Duke of York — a cloth steeped in the innocent blood of his young, pretty son Rutland. The curses that he then from the bitterness of his soul denounced against you have all fallen upon you, and God, not we, has plagued your bloody deed."

Queen Elizabeth said, "God is just when he avenges the innocent."

Hastings said, "Oh, it was the foulest deed to slay that babe, and the most merciless deed that ever was heard of!"

Rivers said, "Tyrants themselves wept when it was reported."

Dorset said, "Every man prophesied that the evil deed would be revenged."

Buckingham said, "Northumberland, who was then present, wept to see it."

The old Queen Margaret replied, "What! Were you all snarling at each other before I came in here, with all of you ready to catch each other by the throat, and now all of you turn all your hatred on me?

"Did the dread curse of Richard's father prevail so much with Heaven that King Henry VI's death, the death of my lovely Prince Edward, the loss of their Kingdom, and my own woeful banishment were all needed to answer for the death of Rutland, that peevish brat?

"Can curses pierce the clouds and enter Heaven the way that prayers can? Why, then, give way, dull clouds, to my quick curses!

"If King Edward IV does not die by war, then may he die from sickness brought on by excess. That will avenge our King — Henry VI — who died from murder in order that your Edward could be made a King!

"Queen Elizabeth, may Edward, your son, who now is Prince of Wales, die just like Edward, my son, who was Prince of Wales, in his youth by similar untimely violence!

"May you, yourself a Queen, to avenge me who was a Queen, outlive your glory, just like my wretched self! Long may you live to mourn the loss of your children, and long may you see another Queen, as I see you now, decked in your rights, as you are installed in mine! May your happy days die long before your death, and, after many lengthened hours of grief, may you die not as a mother, a wife, or as England's Queen!

"Rivers and Dorset, you were bystanders, and so were you, Lord Hastings, when my son, Prince Edward, was stabbed with bloody daggers. I pray to God that none of you may live out your natural life, but that by some unanticipated disaster your loves may be cut short!"

Richard said, "Finish making your curses, you hateful withered hag!"

"And leave you out?" the old Queen Margaret replied. "Stay, dog, for you shall hear me. If Heaven should have any grievous plague in store exceeding those that I can wish upon you, let Heaven keep it until your sins are ripe, and then let Heaven hurl down its indignation on you, the troubler of the poor world's peace! I want you to commit many more sins before you die so that you can be all the more damned to Hell! May the worm of conscience continually gnaw your soul! May you suspect that your friends are traitors while you live, and may you believe that deep traitors are your dearest friends! May no sleep close up your evil eye, unless it be while some tormenting dream frightens you with a Hell of ugly devils! You elvish-marked, abortive and prematurely born, rooting hog! Malignant, spiteful elves marked you with deformities to show that you are their own. You were marked when you were born to show that you are the slave of nature and the son of Hell! You are in bondage to Humankind's fallen nature!"

Margaret began to call Richard names: "You slander of your mother's heavy womb! You loathed issue of your father's loins! You rag of honor! You detested —"

Richard substituted Margaret's name for his own: "— Margaret."

The old Queen Margaret said the correct name: "Richard."

"Ha!" Richard said.

"I am not calling you," she said.

"I beg your mercy then, for I had thought that you had called me all these bitter names."

"Why, so I did, but I looked for no reply. Oh, let me make the period — the end — to my curse!"

"I have already done that," Richard said. "The end of your curse is 'Margaret.'"

Queen Elizabeth said to the old Queen Margaret, "Thus have you made your curse against yourself."

"You are a poor, painted, imitation Queen, a worthless decoration of my throne!" the old Queen Margaret replied. "Why are you strewing sugared words on that bottled spider — that humpbacked Richard — whose deadly web is ensnaring you? Fool, fool! You are sharpening a knife that will be used to kill you. The time will come when you shall wish for me to help you curse that poisonous hunchbacked toad."

Hastings threatened, "You falsely prophesizing woman, end your frantic, insane curse, lest you disturb and end our patience and move us to hurt you."

"Foul shame upon you!" the old Queen Margaret said. "You have all ended my patience."

"Were you well served, and got what you deserved, you would be taught your duty," Rivers said.

The old Queen Margaret replied, "To serve me well, you all should do me duty and show me that I am your Queen and you are my subjects. Oh, serve me well, and teach yourselves to do that duty! You should regard me with reverence!"

"Don't argue with her," the Marquess of Dorset said. "She is a lunatic."

"Be silent, Master Marquess, you are impertinent," the old Queen Margaret said. She was being insulting. "Master" is a title for a boy of good family.

She continued, "Your newly fired stamp of honor is scarcely current — your new honor is like a newly minted coin that has just gone into circulation. Oh, that your young nobility could judge what it were to lose it, and be miserable! They who stand high have many blasts to shake them, and if they fall from their great height, they dash themselves to pieces."

Richard said, "That is good advice, by the Virgin Mary. Learn it, learn it, Marquess of Dorset."

"It touches and concerns you, my lord, as much as me," Dorset said.

"Yes, and much more," Richard said, "but I was born so high. Our brood of young eagles — the sons of my father — build in the cedar's top, and our brood dallies with the wind and scorns the Sun."

Richard was alluding to these proverbs: "The highest trees abide the sharpest winds" and "Only the eagle can gaze at the Sun."

"That brood turns the Sun to shadow," the old Queen Margaret said. "Witness my son, now in the shadow of death, whose bright out-shining beams your cloudy wrath has folded up in eternal darkness. Your brood of young eagles built in the nest of our brood of young eagles. Oh, God, Who sees it, do not endure it! As it was won with blood, so let it also be lost with blood!"

"Stop!" Buckingham said. "Be silent for shame, if not for charity."

"Urge neither charity nor shame to me," the old Queen Margaret replied.

She then said to the people, other than Buckingham, who were present, "Uncharitably with me have you dealt, and shamefully by you my hopes are butchered. The most charitable emotion felt by me is only rage, and the only life I can live is one filled with shame — and in that shame shall always live my sorrows' rage."

"Stop, stop," Buckingham said.

"Oh, Princely Buckingham," the old Queen Margaret said, "I'll kiss your hand as a sign of league and friendship with you. Now may good things happen to you and your noble house! Your garments are not spotted with our blood, nor are you included within the compass of my curse."

"No one else here is included within the compass of your curse," Buckingham said, "for curses never pass the lips of those who breathe them and never go into the air. Curses are not heard by God, and so curses have no effect on those who are cursed."

"I believe that curses ascend the sky, and there they awake God's gentle-sleeping peace," the old Queen Margaret said. "Oh, Buckingham, take heed of yonder dog — Richard! Whenever he fawns, he bites; and when he bites, his venomous tooth creates a festering wound that kills. Have nothing to do with him — beware of him! Sin, death, and Hell have set their marks on him, and all their ministers are his servants."

"What is she saying, my Lord of Buckingham?" Richard asked.

"Nothing that I respect, my gracious lord."

The old Queen Margaret said to Buckingham, "Do you scorn me for my gentle, friendly, kind counsel? And do you soothe and flatter the devil that I warn you against? Oh, just remember this on another day that will come, when he shall split your very heart with sorrow, and then you shall say poor Margaret was a prophetess!"

The old Queen Margaret then said to everyone present, "May each of you live to be the objects of his hate, and may he live to be the objects of your hate, and may all of you live to be the objects of God's hate!"

The old Queen Margaret departed.

Hastings said, "My hair is standing on end from hearing her curses."

"And so is mine," Rivers said. "I wonder why she's at liberty. Why isn't she locked up?"

"I cannot blame her," Richard said. "By God's holy mother, she has had too much wrong done to her, and I repent the wrong that I have done to her."

"I never did her any wrong, to my knowledge," Queen Elizabeth said.

"But you have received all the advantage of the wrongs done to her," Richard said. "I was too hot to do somebody good, who is too cold in thinking about it now."

That somebody was King Edward IV. Richard was saying that he had been eager to make Edward King, but now that Edward was King, Edward was not eager to reward Richard.

Richard continued, "As for Clarence, he is well repaid. He is enclosed in a sty to be fattened up for slaughter in return for his pains, which are similar to my pains. May God pardon all of them who are the cause of Clarence's imprisonment!"

"It is a virtuous and a Christian-like conclusion," Rivers said, "to pray for them who have done injury to us."

Richard replied, "And so I always do."

He thought, *I am well advised to pray for those who do injury, for I am the one who does the injury. If I had cursed those who had gotten Clarence imprisoned, I would have cursed myself.*

Sir William Catesby entered the room and said to Queen Elizabeth, "Madam, his majesty is calling for you."

He then said to Richard and the others, "And he is calling for your grace; and for you, my noble lords."

"Catesby, we are coming," Queen Elizabeth said. "Lords, will you go with us?"

"Madam, we will attend your grace," Rivers replied.

All departed except for Richard, who said to himself, "I do the wrong, and I am the first to begin to quarrel. The secret crimes that I set abroad I lay unto the grievous charge of others.

"Clarence, whom I, indeed, have laid in darkness, I weep over in the presence of many simple, gullible fools, namely, in the presence of Hastings, Lord Stanley, and Buckingham, and say that it is the Queen and her allies who stir the King against the Duke of Clarence, my brother. Now, they believe it, and they urge me to be revenged on Rivers, Vaughan, and Grey — all of whom are allies of Queen Elizabeth.

"But then I sigh, and with a piece of scripture, I tell them that God bids us do good in return for evil, and thus I clothe my naked villainy with old odds and ends stolen out of holy scripture and so I seem to be a saint when I most play the devil."

Two murderers entered the room.

"Quiet!" Richard said to himself. "Here come my executioners."

He said out loud, "How are you now, my hardy, brave determined associates! Are you now going to dispatch this deed?"

"We are, my lord," the first murderer said, "and we have come to get the warrant so that we may be admitted to where he is."

"Good thinking," Richard said. "I have it here on me."

He searched his pockets, pulled out a paper, and looked at it. It was the wrong paper — the one that stated that Clarence was to be released from the Tower of London. He searched another pocket and pulled out another paper — the one that was written earlier than the other paper and stated that

Clarence was to be killed. Richard gave this paper to the first murderer, saying, "When you have finished, go to Crosby Place, a London residence of mine. But, sirs, be quick in the execution, and be obdurate — do not hear him plead for his life, for Clarence is well-spoken, and perhaps he may move your hearts to pity if you listen to him."

The first murderer said, "Tush! Fear not, my lord, we will not stand and make prattling conversation. Talkers are not good doers. Be assured that we have come to use our hands and not our tongues."

"Your eyes drop millstones when fools' eyes drop tears," Richard replied. "I like you lads. Go about your business immediately. Go, go. Hurry."

"We will, my noble lord," the first murderer said.

Clarence and Brakenbury, the Lieutenant of the Tower of London, were in Clarence's cell in the Tower of London.

"Why does your grace look so sad today?" Brakenbury asked.

Clarence replied, "I have passed such a miserable night, so full of ugly sights and ghastly dreams, that, as I am a faithful Christian man, I would not endure another such night even if it would buy me a world of happy days, so full of dismal terror was the miserable night!"

"What was your dream? I want to hear you tell it."

"I thought that I had escaped from the Tower of London and had embarked on a ship to cross to Burgundy, and in my company was my brother, Richard, Duke of Gloucester, who from my cabin persuaded me to walk upon the deck. From there we looked toward England and remembered a thousand fearful times that had befallen us during the wars of the House of York and the House of Lancaster. As we walked along upon the uncertain and unsteady footing of the deck, I thought that Richard stumbled and, in falling, struck me, who tried to steady him, overboard into the tumbling billows of the ocean.

"Lord! Lord! I thought what pain it was to drown! What a dreadful noise of waters was in my ears! What ugly sights of death were within my eyes!

"I thought I saw a thousand dreadful shipwrecks, ten thousand men whom fishes gnawed upon, ingots of gold, great anchors, heaps of pearls, precious stones, and jewels that were precious beyond anyone's ability to judge their worth — all scattered on the bottom of the sea. Some lay in dead men's skulls; and, in those holes where eyes did once inhabit, there were crept, as if in scorn of eyes, reflecting gems, which wooed the slimy bottom of the deep, and mocked the dead bones that lay scattered nearby."

Brakenbury asked, "Had you such leisure in your time of death to gaze upon the secrets of the deep?"

"I thought I had," Clarence said, "and often I strove to yield my soul, but always the malignant flood of water kept my soul in my body, and would not let it go forth to seek the empty, vast, and wandering air; instead, the ocean smothered my soul within my panting body, which almost burst in its attempt to belch my soul into the sea."

"Didn't you wake up because of this heavy anguish?"

"No, my dream continued after my life ended in my dream. Then began the tempest to my soul, which passed, I thought, over the melancholy River Styx with that grim ferryman — Charon — whom poets write about, and into the kingdom of perpetual night — Hell.

"The first there who did greet my newly arrived soul was my great father-in-law, the renowned Earl of Warwick, who cried aloud, 'What scourge for perjury can this dark monarchy give false Clarence?' And then he vanished.

"Next came wandering by a shadow like an angel, with bright hair daubed in blood; and he shrieked out loud, 'Clarence has come — false, fickle, perjured Clarence, who stabbed me in the battlefield by Tewksbury. Seize him, Furies, and take him to your torments!'"

The shadow like an angel was Prince Edward, whom Clarence had helped kill in the Battle of Tewksbury. Prince Edward was calling on the Furies — ancient Greek avenging goddesses — to torment Clarence.

Clarence continued, "With that, I thought, a legion of foul fiends surrounded me, and howled in my ears such hideous cries that with the noise I awakened trembling, and for a time afterward could not but believe that I was in Hell, such a terrible impression the dream made on me."

"It is no wonder, my lord, that the dream frightened you," Brakenbury said. "I promise you that I was afraid when I heard you tell it."

"Oh, Brakenbury, I have done things that now bear evidence against my soul — things I did for the sake of my brother Edward, and see how he repays me!" Clarence said.

He prayed, "Oh, God, if my deep prayers cannot appease You, but You must be avenged on my misdeeds, yet execute Your wrath on me alone and spare my guiltless wife and my poor children!"

He said to Brakenbury, "Please, gentle jailor, stay by me. My soul is heavy — sorrowful and tired — and I wish to sleep."

"I will, my lord," Brakenbury replied. "May God give your grace a good rest!"

Clarence fell asleep.

Brakenbury said to himself, "Sorrow interrupts seasons and the hours for sleeping, makes the night morning, and makes the noontime night. Princes have only their titles for their glories, outward honors for inward toils, and in return for the satisfactions that Princes are thought to enjoy, but do not, Princes often feel a world of restless cares. The conclusion is that, between the titles of Princes and the names of commoners, there's no difference except the outward fame."

The two murderers entered the cell.

"Ho! Who's here?" the first murderer asked.

"In God's name who and what are you," Brakenbury asked, "and how did you come here?"

"I am a man who wants to speak with Clarence, and I came here on my legs," the first murderer replied.

"Must you be so brief?" Brakenbury asked.

"Sir, it is better to be brief than tedious," the second murderer replied.

The second murderer then said to the first murderer, "Show him our commission; talk no more."

Brakenbury read the commission and said, "I am by this commission ordered to deliver the noble Duke of Clarence into your hands. I will not reason about what is meant by this because I want to be guiltless and not know the meaning. Here are the keys, there sits the Duke asleep. I'll go to the King and inform him that I have resigned my charge to you."

"Do so, it is a wise thing to do," the first murderer said. "Fare you well."

Brakenbury departed.

The second murderer asked about Clarence, "What, shall we stab him as he sleeps?"

"No; if we do that, then he will say it was done cowardly, when he wakes up," the first murderer said.

"When he wakes up! Why, fool, he shall never wake up until Judgment Day."

"Why, at that time he will say we stabbed him while he was sleeping."

"The urging of that word 'judgment' has bred a kind of remorse in me," the second murderer said.

"Are you afraid?"

"I am not afraid to kill him, since we have a warrant for it, but I am afraid of being damned to Hell for killing him. On Judgment Day, no warrant can defend us."

"I thought you were resolute and resolved," the first murderer said.

"So I am, but not to commit this murder. I am resolute and resolved to let Clarence live."

"Go back to Richard, Duke of Gloucester, and tell him that."

"Please, wait a while," the second murderer said. "I hope my holy mood will change; it usually keeps hold of me only until a man can count to twenty."

"How do you feel now?"

"Truly, I have some dregs of conscience still inside me."

"Remember the reward we will get when the deed is done," the first murderer said.

"By God's wounds, Clarence dies," the second murderer said. "I had forgotten about the reward."

"Where is your conscience now?"

"In Richard, Duke of Gloucester's purse."

"So when he opens his purse to give us our reward," the first murderer said, "your conscience will fly out."

"Let it go; there's few or none who will welcome it."

"What if it comes to you again?" the first murderer asked.

"I'll not meddle with it; it is a dangerous thing. A conscience makes a man a coward. A man cannot steal, but his conscience accuses him. He cannot swear, but it stops him. He cannot lie with his neighbor's wife, but it detects him. A conscience is a blushing, shame-faced spirit that mutinies in a man's bosom; it fills a man full of obstacles. My conscience once made me restore a purse of gold that I found; a conscience beggars any man who keeps it. A conscience is turned out of all towns and cities because it is a dangerous thing, and every man who means to live well endeavors to trust to himself and to live without it."

"By God's wounds, my conscience is even now at my elbow, persuading me not to kill the Duke of Clarence," the first murderer said.

"Arrest the devil — your conscience — in your mind, and do not let him loose; the devil wants to curry favor with you only in order to make you sigh."

"Tut, I am strong-framed; he cannot prevail with me, I promise you."

"Spoken like a brave fellow who respects his reputation," the second murderer said. "Come, shall we fall to work?"

"Hit him on the head with the hilt of your sword, and then we will throw him in the barrel of sweet malmsey wine in the next room and drown him."

"Oh, excellent plan!" the second murderer said. "We will make a sop of him."

A sop is a piece of cake or bread soaked in wine.

"Listen," the first murderer said. "He is waking up and stirring. Shall I strike him?"

"No, first let's talk with him," the first murderer said.

"Where are you, jail keeper?" Clarence said. "Give me a cup of wine."

"You shall have wine soon enough, my lord," the second murderer said.

"In God's name, who are you?" Clarence asked.

"A man, as you are," the second murderer replied.

"But you are not, as I am, royal," Clarence said.

"Nor are you, as we are, loyal," the second murderer said.

"Your voice is thunderous, but your looks show you to be a commoner," Clarence said.

"My voice is now King Edward IV's, my looks are my own," the second murderer said.

"How darkly and how deadly do you speak!" Clarence said. "Your eyes menace me. Why do you look pale? Who sent you here? Why have you come?"

Both murderers stuttered, "To, to, to —"

Clarence finished for them, "To murder me?"

Both murderers said, "Yes, yes."

"You scarcely have the hearts to tell me so, and therefore you cannot have the hearts to do it," Clarence said. "In what, my friends, have I offended you?"

The first murderer said, "You have not offended us, but you have offended King Edward IV."

"I shall be reconciled to him again," Clarence said.

"Never, my lord," the second murderer said, "so prepare to die."

"Are you handpicked from out of the entire world of men to slay the innocent?" Clarence asked. "What is my offence? Where are the witnesses who accuse me? What lawful jury has given its verdict to the frowning judge? Or who has pronounced the bitter sentence of poor Clarence's death?

"To threaten me with death before I have been convicted by the course of law is most unlawful. I command you, as you hope to have redemption by Christ's dear blood that was shed for our grievous sins, to depart and lay no hands on me. The deed you undertake is damnable — if you commit it, you will be damned to Hell."

"What we will do, we do upon command," the first murderer replied.

"And he who has commanded us to do it is the King," the second murderer said.

"Mistaken wretches!" Clarence said. "The great King of Kings has in the tablets of his law — the Ten Commandments — commanded that you shall commit no murder. Will you, then, spurn and reject contemptuously God's command and carry out the command of a mere man? Take heed; for God holds vengeance in His hands, and He will hurl His vengeance upon the heads of those who break His law."

The second murderer said, "And that same vengeance God hurls on you, for false forswearing and for murder, too. You took an oath on the Holy Eucharist to fight on behalf of the House of Lancaster."

The first murderer said, "And, like a traitor to the name of God, you broke that vow; and with your treacherous blade you laid open the bowels of your sovereign's son. You fought for your Yorkist brother Edward, and you murdered Prince Edward, the Lancastrian son of King Henry VI."

"You had sworn to cherish and defend Prince Edward."

"How can you urge God's dreadful law against us, when you have broken it in such a significant degree?"

"Alas!" Clarence said. "For whose sake did I do that ill deed? I did it for Edward, for my brother, for his sake. Why, sirs, he sends you not to murder me for this because in this sin he is as deep as I. If God will be revenged for this deed, you should know that He will do it publicly. Do not take the cause of complaint and the punishment for the sin away from God's powerful arm; God needs no devious or lawless course to cut off those who have offended Him."

The first murderer asked Clarence, "Who made you, then, a bloody agent, when the finely growing, splendid, lively, and brave Plantagenet — Prince Edward, that Princely youth — was struck dead by you?"

"Who made me a bloody agent? My brother's love, the devil, and my rage," Clarence answered.

"Your brother's 'love,' our duty, and your sin," the first murderer said, "provoke us here and now to slaughter you."

The brother the first murderer referred to was Richard, but Clarence thought that he meant Edward.

"Oh, if you love my brother, do not hate me," Clarence said. "I am his brother, and I love him well. If you are hired for a reward, go back again, and I will send you to my brother Richard, Duke of Gloucester, who shall reward you better for my life than Edward will for tidings of my death."

"You are deceived," the second murderer said. "Your brother Richard, Duke of Gloucester, hates you."

"Oh, no, he loves me, and he holds me dear," Clarence said. "Go from me to him."

Both murderers replied, "Yes, we will."

They meant that after they had murdered Clarence, they would go to Richard and collect their reward for committing the murder.

"Tell Richard that when our Princely father the Duke of York blessed his three sons with his victorious arm, and charged us from his soul to love each other, he little thought of this divided friendship," Clarence said. "He did not think that the friendship between us three brothers would be broken. Tell my brother Richard to think of this, and he will weep."

"Yes, he will weep," the first murderer said. "He will weep millstones instead of tears, just as he taught us to weep."

"Do not slander Richard, for he is kind," Clarence said.

"Right, he is kind," the first murderer said. "He is as kind as snow during harvest time. You deceive yourself. Richard is the man who sent us here now to slaughter you."

"It cannot be," Clarence said, "for when I parted with him, he hugged me in his arms, and he swore, with sobs, that he would labor to bring about my delivery from the Tower of London."

"Why, so he does," the second murderer said. "Even now he delivers you from this world's bondage to the joys of Heaven."

The first murderer said, "Make peace with God, for you must die, my lord."

"Have you that holy feeling in your soul that you counsel me to make my peace with God, and are you yet to your own soul so blind that you will war with God by murdering me?" Clarence replied. "Ah, sirs, consider, the man who set you on to do this deed will hate you for the deed."

"What shall we do?" the second murderer asked.

"Relent, and save your souls," Clarence replied.

"Relent!" the first murderer said. "That would be cowardly and womanish."

"Not to relent is beastly, savage, devilish," Clarence said. "Which of you, if you were a Prince's son, being imprisoned away from liberty, as I am now, if two such murderers as yourselves came to you, would not beg for life?"

Clarence said to the second murderer, "My friend, I see some pity in your looks. Oh, if your eye is not a flatterer, come and be on my side, and beg for me, as you would beg if you were in my distressful situation. What beggar will not pity a begging Prince?"

The second murderer relented and tried to warn Clarence: "Look behind you, my lord!"

The first murderer stabbed Clarence a few times as he said, "Take that, and that. If all this will not kill you, I'll drown you in the barrel of malmsey wine inside this other room."

The first murderer carried the still-breathing Clarence out of the cell.

The second murderer said to himself, "A bloody deed, and desperately dispatched! How I would like to, like Pontius Pilate, wash my hands of this most grievous and guilty murder!"

Pontius Pilate had reluctantly allowed the crucifixion of Jesus to take place, but he had washed his hands in an attempt to show that he was not taking responsibility for his act.

The first murderer returned and said to the second murderer, "Hey! Why didn't you help me to murder Clarence? By Heavens, Richard shall know how slack you have been!"

"I wish that Richard could know that I had saved the life of his brother, but that did not happen!" the second murderer replied. "You take the fee for committing the murder, and tell Richard what I just said, for I repent and I am sorry that the Duke of Clarence has been slain."

The second murderer exited.

The first murderer said, "I do not repent the murder. Go, coward that you are. Now I must hide Clarence's body in some hole, until Richard, Duke of Gloucester, makes an order for his burial. And when I have my reward for committing the murder, I must run away, for this murder will out — murders do not remain hidden — and here I must not stay."

CHAPTER 2

— 2.1 —

In a room of the palace were an ill King Edward IV, Queen Elizabeth, Dorset, Rivers, Hastings, Buckingham, Grey, and others. Two factions were represented in this group of people. One faction consisted of Queen Elizabeth, Dorset, Rivers, and Grey; Hastings and Buckingham had been opposed to this faction. King Edward IV was working to reconcile these factions.

King Edward IV said, "Why, good; now I have done a good day's work. You peers, continue this united league. I every day expect a message from my Redeemer to redeem me from this world, and now my soul shall part in peace from Earth and go to Heaven, since I have set my friends at peace on Earth. Rivers and Hastings, take each other's hand. Do not hide any hatred and pretend to be reconciled; instead, sincerely swear your friendship for each other."

Rivers said, "By Heaven, my heart has purged all grudging hate, and with my hand I seal my true heart's friendship for Hastings."

Hastings shook Rivers' hand and said, "May I prosper, as I truly swear my true heart's friendship for Rivers!"

King Edward IV said, "Take heed you do not put on an act before your Earthly King, lest He who is the Supreme King of Kings put to shame your hidden falsehood and make each of you the death of the other."

Hastings said, "May I prosper, as I swear perfect friendship! May I thrive according to the truth of my swearing. If I am lying, may God keep me from thriving. If I am telling the truth, may God let me thrive."

"And may I prosper, as I swear that I regard Hastings as my friend with all my heart!" Rivers said.

King Edward IV said to his wife, Queen Elizabeth, "Madam, you yourself are not exempt in this, nor is your son Dorset, nor Buckingham, nor you, Hastings. All of you have been in one faction that is opposed against the other. Wife, respect Lord Hastings, let him kiss your hand, and when you do it, do it honestly."

"Here, Hastings," Queen Elizabeth said, giving Hastings her hand. "I will never any more remember our former hatred, so thrive I and mine! May I thrive according to the truth of my swearing."

Hastings kissed her hand.

"Marquess of Dorset, embrace Hastings; Hastings, respect the Lord Marquess of Dorset," King Edward IV said.

Dorset said, "This interchange of respect, I here promise, upon my part shall be inviolable."

"And I swear the same, my lord," Hastings said.

Dorset and Hastings hugged each other.

King Edward IV said, "Now, Princely Buckingham, seal this league by embracing my wife's allies, and make me happy in your unity."

Buckingham said to Queen Elizabeth, "Whenever Buckingham turns his hate on you or yours, and unless with all duteous love Buckingham cherishes you and yours, may God punish me with hatred of me in those whom I most expect to love and respect me! If I ever turn my hatred against you or yours, then when I have the most need to employ a friend, and when I am most assured that he is a friend, let him be deeply cunning, hollow, treacherous, and full of guile to me. Let him betray me! I beg of God to let this happen if I am ever cold in zeal to you and your family."

"Your vow is a pleasing cordial — a restorative — to my sickly heart," King Edward IV said. "Now we need only our brother Richard, Duke of Gloucester, here to make the perfect end to this making of peace."

Seeing Richard coming toward them, Buckingham said, "And, at exactly the right time, here comes the noble Duke of Gloucester."

Richard said, "Good morning to my sovereign King and Queen, and, Princely peers, I wish you a happy time of day!"

King Edward IV said, "This day has been happy, indeed, because of how we have spent the day."

Using the royal plural, he said, "Brother, we have done deeds of Christian charity; we have made peace out of enmity and fair love out of hate, between these swollen-with-anger and wrongly incensed peers."

"That is a blessed labor, my most sovereign liege," Richard said. "Amongst this Princely heap of nobles, if there is anyone here who because of bad information or incorrect surmises thinks that I am a foe, and if I unwittingly, or in my rage, have committed anything that is endured only with great difficulty by anyone here present before the King, I desire to be reconciled to that person and to his friendly peace. It is death to me to be involved in enmity; I hate hatred, and I desire all good men's friendship.

"First, madam, Queen Elizabeth, I entreat true peace from you, which I will purchase with my duteous service.

"From you, my noble cousin Buckingham, I entreat true peace if ever any grudge were lodged between us.

"From you, Lord Rivers, and, Lord Grey, from you, I entreat true peace. You two have frowned on me without any merit.

"Dukes, Earls, lords, gentlemen — indeed, I entreat true peace from all.

"I do not know any Englishman alive with whom my soul is even a little bit more at odds than the Englishman will be with the infant who is born tonight.

"I thank my God for my humility."

Queen Elizabeth said, "This day shall be remembered hereafter as a holy day. I wish to God all contentious arguments could be as well ended."

She said to her husband, "My sovereign liege, I beg your majesty to show mercy to our brother-in-law Clarence."

Richard said, "Why, madam, have I offered friendship for this — to be so abused and mocked in the royal presence of the King? Who does not know that the noble Duke of Clarence is dead?"

Everyone was startled by the news.

Richard continued, "You do him wrong to scorn his corpse."

Rivers said, "'Who does not know that the noble Duke of Clarence is dead?' Who knows that he is dead?"

"All-seeing Heaven, what a world is this!" Queen Elizabeth said.

"Do I look as pale, Lord Dorset, as the others who are here?" Buckingham asked.

"Yes, my good lord; there is no one here in the presence of the King who has not had the red color forsake his cheeks. All of us are pale," Dorset said.

"Is Clarence dead?" King Edward IV asked. "I revoked the order to have him killed."

"But Clarence, poor soul, died by your first order," Richard said. "The order to have Clarence killed was carried by a winged Mercury, the quick messenger of the gods. Some tardy cripple carried the second order, which countermanded the first order. That tardy cripple lagged and came too late even to see Clarence buried."

Richard was capable of black humor. The tardy cripple who carried the second order was himself.

Richard continued, "May God grant that some people, who are less noble and less loyal than Clarence, who are more bloody than him in their thoughts but who are not as royal in their blood relations, do not deserve even worse treatment than wretched Clarence did — and yet they are thought to be true citizens and are unsuspected of any wrongdoing!"

Lord Stanley, Earl of Derby, entered the room and said to King Edward IV, "I ask for a boon, my sovereign, in return for the service I have done for you!"

"Please, leave me in peace," King Edward IV replied. "My soul is full of sorrow."

Lord Stanley knelt and said, "I will not rise, unless your highness grants me the favor I ask for."

"Then tell me at once what it is you demand," King Edward IV replied.

"My servant has forfeited his life because he slew today a righteous gentleman who was recently an attendant of the Duke of Norfolk. I want you to save my servant's life."

"Do I have a tongue that doomed my brother Clarence to death, and shall that same tongue give pardon to a slave?" King Edward IV said. "My brother slew no man; his crime was only in his thoughts, and yet his punishment was cruel death. Who sued to me to pardon his life? Who, when I was angry at him, knelt at my feet, and asked me to think things over and be judicious and prudent? Who spoke to me of brotherhood? Who spoke to me of love? Who reminded me of how Clarence, that poor soul, forsook the mighty Earl of Warwick, and instead fought for me? Who reminded me that, in the battlefield by Tewksbury when the Earl of Oxford had me down, he rescued me and said, 'Dear brother, live, and be a King'? Who reminded me that, when we both lay in the field frozen almost to death, how he wrapped me in his own garments, and exposed himself, all thinly clothed and practically naked, to the numbingly cold night?

"All these things brutish wrath sinfully plucked from my memory, and not a man of you had enough grace to remind me of them. But when your wagon drivers or your waiting-servants have committed a drunken slaughter, and defaced the precious image of our dear Redeemer by killing a man who was created in His image, you immediately get on your knees and beg for pardon, and I — who am unjust, too — must grant it to you.”

Lord Stanley stood up.

King Edward IV continued, “But not a man would speak up for my brother Clarence. Nor did I, ungracious as I am, speak to myself on behalf of him, poor soul. The proudest of you all have been beholden to him during his life, yet none of you would plead even once for his life.

“Oh, God, I fear Your justice will destroy me, and all of these men here, and my family members, and their family members, because of this!

“Come, Hastings, help me to my private room.

“Oh, poor Clarence!”

King Edward IV, Queen Elizabeth, and most of the others left the room.

Richard, Hastings, and Buckingham remained behind.

Richard said, “This is the fruit of rashness! Did you see how the guilty relatives of the Queen looked pale when they heard about Clarence’s death?”

True, the relatives of Queen Elizabeth had looked pale, but everyone had looked pale when they learned of Clarence’s death.

Richard continued, “Oh, they continually urged the King to kill him! God will revenge it. But come, let us go in, so we can comfort Edward with our company.”

Buckingham said, “We will go with you, your grace.”

The old Duchess of York was in a room of the palace with Clarence's two children, a boy and a girl. The old Duchess of York was the children's grandmother; she was the mother of King Edward IV, Clarence, and Richard.

Clarence's young son asked the old Duchess of York, "Tell me, good grandmother, is our father dead?"

"No, boy," she lied.

He asked, "Why then do you wring your hands, and beat your breast, and cry, 'Oh, Clarence, my unhappy son!'"

Clarence's young daughter asked her, "Why do you look on us, and shake your head, and call us wretches, orphans, and castaways, if our noble father is still alive?"

The old Duchess of York said, "My pretty grandchildren, you are much mistaken about me; I lament the sickness of King Edward IV. I am loath to lose him. I am not lamenting your father's death; it is lost sorrow to cry for one who's lost. When someone has died, it is useless to mourn him."

"Then, grandmother, you are saying that our father is dead," Clarence's son said. "King Edward IV, my uncle, is to blame for this. God will revenge it; I will beg Him to revenge my father's death in my daily prayers."

"And so will I," Clarence's daughter said.

"Peace, children, peace!" the old Duchess of York said. "King Edward IV loves you well. Uncomprehending and naive innocents, you cannot guess who caused your father's death."

Clarence's son said, "Grandmother, we can because my good uncle Richard, Duke of Gloucester, told me that the King, provoked by the Queen, devised charges on which to imprison him. And when my uncle Richard told me that, he wept, and hugged me in his arms, and kindly kissed my cheek. He told me to rely on him as I would rely on my father, and he told me that he would love me as dearly as if I were his child."

"Oh, that deceit should steal such a gentle and friendly disguise, and with a virtuous mask hide foul guile!" the old Duchess of York said. "He is my son, yes, and therein he is my shame. Yet from my breasts he did not drink this deceitfulness with his milk when he was a baby."

"Do you think that my uncle Richard was lying, grandmother?" the boy asked.

"Yes, boy."

"I cannot think that is true," he said. "Listen! What is that noise?"

A grieving Queen Elizabeth, with her hair loose about her ears, entered the room. Her son Dorset followed her; so did Rivers, her brother.

"Oh, who shall stop me from wailing and weeping, from berating my fortune, and from tormenting myself?" Queen Elizabeth said. "I'll join with black despair against my soul, and to myself I will become an enemy. I will despair and commit suicide."

The old Duchess of York asked, "What do you mean by making this scene of barbarous lack of self-control? Why are you making such a scene?"

"I mean to make an act of tragic violence," Queen Elizabeth said. "Edward IV, my lord and husband, your son, our King, is dead. Why do the branches grow now that the root is withered? Why don't the leaves wither now that the sap is gone? If you will continue to live, lament; if you will die, be quick, so that our swift-winged souls may catch the King's soul, or so that, like obedient subjects, we may follow him to his new Kingdom of perpetual rest."

"Ah, so much interest have I in your sorrow as I had title in your noble husband!" the old Duchess of York said. "I have wept because of the death of a worthy husband, and lived by looking on his images — his children. But now two mirrors of his Princely semblance — two of my husband's children, Edward and Clarence — are cracked in pieces by malignant death, and I for comfort have only one false mirror, Richard, who grieves me when I look at him and feel shame.

"You are a widow; yet you are a mother, and you have the comfort of your children left to you. But death has snatched my husband from my arms, and plucked two crutches from my feeble limbs — those crutches are Edward and Clarence. Since your grief is only half of my grief, I have cause enough to surpass you in grieving and drown out your cries of grief!"

Clarence's son said to Queen Elizabeth, "Good aunt, you did not weep for our father's death. How then can we justify aiding you with our familial tears by crying for the death of your husband?"

Clarence's daughter said, "Our fatherless distress was left unwept by you; may your widow's grief likewise be unwept by us!"

"Give me no help in lamentation," Queen Elizabeth said, weeping. "I am not barren in bringing forth complaints — I am pregnant with sorrow. May all springs direct their currents to my eyes, so that I, being governed by the watery Moon, may send forth tears enough to drown the world! I cry for my husband, for my dear lord, Edward!"

Weeping, Clarence's children said, "We cry for our father, for our dear lord, Clarence!"

Weeping, the old Duchess of York said, "I cry for both, for both are mine, Edward and Clarence!"

"What support had I but Edward?" Queen Elizabeth said, "And he's dead and gone."

Clarence's children said, "What support had we but our father, Clarence? And he's dead and gone."

"What supports had I but my sons Edward and Clarence?" the old Duchess of York said. "And they are dead and gone."

"Never has a widow had so dear a loss!" Queen Elizabeth said.

"Never have orphans had so dear a loss!" Clarence's children said.

"Never has a mother had so dear a loss!" the old Duchess of York said. "I am the mother of these men we grieve! Your woes are for an individual death; my woes are for both deaths! Queen Elizabeth weeps for Edward IV, and so do I; I weep for Clarence, but she does not. These babes weep for Clarence and so do I; I weep for Edward, and they do not.

"I am more distressed than the three of you, so you three ought to pour all your tears on me. I am your sorrow's wet nurse, and I will feed sorrow with my lamentations."

Dorset said, "Be comforted, dear mother: God is much displeased that you take with ungratefulness what is His doing. In common worldly things, when we with sullen unwillingness repay a debt that with a bounteous hand was kindly lent, we are called ungrateful. We are all the more ungrateful when we oppose Heaven, which lent you King Edward IV, and now has required that the royal debt be repaid."

Rivers said, "Madam, think, like a careful and concerned mother, of the young Prince Edward, your son. Send immediately for him and let him be crowned; in him your comfort lives. Drown your desperate sorrow in dead

Edward's grave, and plant your joys in living Edward's throne. King Edward IV is dead; Edward, Prince of Wales, lives."

Richard, Buckingham, Lord Stanley, Hastings, and Sir Richard Ratcliff entered the room.

Richard said to Queen Elizabeth, "Madam, be comforted. All of us have cause to grieve the dimming of our shining star, Edward IV, but none can cure their harms by grieving them."

He then said to the old Duchess of York, "Madam, my mother, I beg your pardon. I did not see your grace."

He knelt and said, "Humbly on my knee I ask for your blessing."

The old Duchess of York said, "May God bless you and put meekness in your mind, as well as love, charity, obedience, and true duty!"

Richard said, "Amen," as he stood up.

He thought, *And let God make me die a good old man! That ought to be the conclusion of a mother's blessing. I wonder why her grace left it out.*

Buckingham said, "You gloomy Princes and heart-sorrowing peers, who bear this mutual heavy load of moaning grief, cheer up each other now in each other's love. Though we have spent our harvest of this King, we are yet to reap the harvest of his son. The broken rancor of your high-swollen hearts — rancor just recently broken, splinted, knit, and joined together like a barely healed broken leg — must gently be preserved, cherished, and kept."

Most of Buckingham's listeners thought that he had meant to say this: We must ensure that the rancor remains broken so that peace can be the result. But the content of what he had said was ambiguous. He could have meant this: We must ensure that the rancor — which was recently broken — between us remains.

Buckingham added, "It seems to be a good idea that with some little train of followers the young Prince of Wales be fetched here to London, so that he can be crowned our King."

"Why with some little — not great — train of followers, my Lord of Buckingham?" Rivers asked.

"My lord, I am afraid that if a multitude of followers bring the Prince out of Wales that the newly healed wound of malice could break out and factions could form again and quarrel. This danger is all the more likely because the new state is green and newly established and as yet ungoverned — we have not yet crowned the new King. In such a state every horse bears the reins that should command it, and every horse may direct its course as it pleases. In my opinion, we ought to prevent both real harm as well as the fear that real harm may occur."

Rivers listened, and he thought that Buckingham was pointing out that if a large number of people who had recently been in opposing factions got together to escort the Prince of Wales to London, it was possible that their close proximity could cause quarrels to break out. It was better to prevent that possibility by having a small train of followers escort the Prince. A small train of followers could more easily control themselves. In addition, if a large train of followers included a large number of people who had been in the faction opposing Queen Elizabeth, they could stage a coup and not allow her son the Prince to be crowned King.

Rivers did not reflect that if a small train of followers escorted the Prince, and that small train of followers was the faction opposing Queen Elizabeth, it could seek to control the Prince.

Richard said, "I hope King Edward IV made peace with all of us, and the agreement we made to be friends with each other is firm and true. I know that it is firm and true in me."

"As it is in me," Rivers said, "and so, I think, in all of us. Yet, since the state is still green, it should be put to no apparent likelihood of breach, which perhaps by much company might be urged: We don't want a coup to take power from the Prince of Wales. Therefore, I say with noble Buckingham, that it is fitting only a few people should fetch the Prince."

"I agree," Hastings said.

Richard said, "Then let it be so, and let us determine who shall be the men who immediately shall ride to Ludlow to meet the Prince."

He said to Queen Elizabeth and the old Duchess of York, "Madam, and you, my mother, will you go with us so you can give your advice in this important business?"

Both replied together, "With all our hearts."

Everyone departed except for Richard and Buckingham.

Buckingham said, "My lord, whoever journeys to meet the Prince and escort him to London, for God's sake, let us two not be left behind, for, along the road, I'll find an occasion, as the beginning to the plot we recently talked about, to part the Queen's proud relatives from the Prince, who will be the new King."

Richard replied, "You are my other self, my source of excellent advice, my oracle, my prophet! My dear kinsman, I, as if I were a child, will guide myself by your advice. Towards Ludlow we will ride, for we'll not stay behind."

On a street, two citizens talked together.

The first citizen said, "Neighbor, we are well met. Where are you going so quickly?"

"I assure you, I scarcely know myself," the second citizen said. "Have you heard the news that is going around?"

"Yes, that King Edward IV is dead."

"That is bad news; seldom comes good news. I fear our world will prove to be troubled."

A third citizen arrived and said, "Neighbors, may God make you prosper!"

"Good morning, sir," the first citizen replied.

The third citizen asked, "Is this news of good King Edward IV's death true?"

The second citizen said, "Yes, sir, it is too true; may God help the times!"

"Since it is true," the third citizen said, "then, masters, look to see a troubled world."

"No, no," the first citizen said. "By God's good grace, King Edward IV's son shall reign."

"Woe to the land that's governed by a child!" the third citizen said.

The second citizen said, "In him there is a hope of good government. His council of advisors will govern well while he is a minor, and in his full and mature years he himself, no doubt, shall govern well."

"So stood the state when King Henry VI was crowned in Paris when he was only nine months old."

"Stood the state so?" the third citizen said. "No, no, good friends, God knows that the situations are different. For then this land was famously enriched with prudent and grave counsel; King Henry VI had virtuous uncles to protect his grace."

"Why, so has our own Prince of Wales," the first citizen said. "He has good advisors on both his father's and his mother's side."

The third citizen said, "It would be better if they all were on the father's side, or if none at all came from the father's side. But now there are factions, and they will compete about who shall be nearest to the new King Edward V. Their competition for power will touch and hurt us all too dearly, if God does not prevent it. The Duke of Gloucester is very dangerous! And Queen Elizabeth's sons and brothers are haughty and proud. If both sides were to be ruled, and not to rule, this sickly land might feel solace as it has before. Now we are likely to have a struggle for power."

"Come, come, we fear the worst," the first citizen said, "but all shall be well."

"Wise men are prepared," the third citizen said. "When clouds appear, wise men put on their cloaks. When great leaves fall, the winter is at hand. When the Sun sets, who doesn't expect night? Untimely storms make men expect a dearth of food. All may be well, but if God arranged all to be well, it is more than we deserve, or I expect."

The second citizen said, "Truly, the souls of men are full of dread. It is difficult to find a man to talk to who does not look serious and full of fear."

"Before times of change, it is always like this," the third citizen said. "By a divine instinct, men's minds predict ensuing dangers; as by experience, we see the waters of the sea swell before a boisterous storm. But let's leave it all to God. Where are you going?"

The second citizen said, "The justices sent for us."

"They also sent for me," the third citizen said. "I'll go with you and keep you company."

— 2.4 —

In a room in the palace were the Archbishop of York, the young Duke of York, Queen Elizabeth, and the old Duchess of York.

The young Duke of York was the Prince of Wales' younger brother. Both were the sons of Queen Elizabeth and King Edward IV.

"Last night, I hear, they spent the night at Northampton," the Archbishop of York said. "They will be at Stony Stratford tonight. Tomorrow, or the day after tomorrow they will be here."

The old Duchess of York said, "I long with all my heart to see the Prince of Wales. I hope he has grown much since I last saw him."

Queen Elizabeth said, "But I hear that he has not grown much; they say my son the young Duke of York has almost grown as tall as he is."

"Yes, mother, but I would not have it so," the young Duke of York said.

"Why, my young grandson, it is good to grow," the old Duchess of York said.

"Grandmother, one night, as we sat down for supper, my uncle Rivers talked about how I was growing taller than my brother. 'Yes,' said my uncle Richard, Duke of Gloucester, 'small herbs have grace, great weeds do grow apace.' And since then I have hoped I would not grow so fast, because sweet flowers grow slowly and weeds grow hastily."

"Truly, the saying did not hold true for him who told you the saying," the old Duchess of York said. "Richard was the most wretched thing when he was young. He grew very slowly and very leisurely. If this saying were true, Richard would be a gracious man."

"Why, madam, so, no doubt, he is," the Archbishop of York said politely.

"I hope he is," the old Duchess of York said. "But I am his mother, and I have my doubts."

"Now, truly," the young Duke of York said, "if I had remembered, I could have made a jest that would hit my uncle Richard's growth harder than he hit mine."

"How would you do that, my pretty grandson of York?" the old Duchess of York said. "Please, let me hear it."

55

"They say that my uncle Richard grew so fast that he could gnaw a crust when he was two hours old. It was two full years before I had my first tooth. Grandmother, this would have been a biting jest."

"Please, my pretty grandson of York, who told you this?" the old Duchess of York asked.

"Grandmother, Richard's nurse told me," the young Duke of York replied.

"His nurse! Why, she was dead before you were born."

"If she didn't tell me, then I don't know who told me."

"You are a precocious boy," Queen Elizabeth said. "You are too shrewd and clever for your own good."

"Good madam, don't be angry with the child," the Archbishop of York said.

"Pitchers have ears," Queen Elizabeth said. She meant that her son had been listening to the gossip of adults.

A messenger entered the room.

"Here comes a messenger," the Archbishop of York said. "What is the news?"

"I have such bad news, my lord, that it grieves me to tell it to you."

Immediately worried about her other son by King Edward IV, Queen Elizabeth asked, "How is the Prince of Wales?"

"He is well, madam," the messenger said. "He is in good health."

"What is your news then?" the old Duchess of York asked.

"Lord Rivers and Lord Grey have been sent to Pomfret Castle, as has Sir Thomas Vaughan; they are prisoners."

Pomfret Castle was in northern England. King Richard II and other political prisoners had been killed there.

"Who has committed them there?" the old Duchess of York asked.

"Two mighty Dukes: Gloucester and Buckingham."

"For what offence?" Queen Elizabeth asked.

Rivers was her brother; Grey was her son; Vaughan was her ally.

"The sum of everything I know, I have told you," the messenger said. "Why or for what these nobles were sent to prison is entirely unknown to me, my gracious lady."

Queen Elizabeth said, "I see the downfall and ruin of our House, our family! The tiger now has seized the gentle doe. Contemptuously exulting tyranny begins to encroach upon the innocent throne, on which sits King

Edward V, who is so young that he does not awe his subjects. Welcome, destruction, death, and massacre! I see, as in a map or picture, the end of all."

The old Duchess of York said, "Accursed and unquiet wrangling days, how many of you have my eyes beheld! My husband lost his life in an attempt to get the crown, and often my sons were tossed up and down on the Wheel of Fortune over their losses. Once King Edward IV was seated on the throne, and domestic quarrels had entirely abated, the conquering faction made war upon each other. It was blood relative against blood relative, and self against self. Oh, monstrous, perverted, and frantic outrage, end your damned malice, or let me die so I do not look on death any longer!"

Queen Elizabeth said to her son, "Come, come, my boy; we will go to sanctuary in Westminster Abbey. We are in danger."

She said to the old Duchess of York, "Madam, farewell."

"I'll go along with you," she replied.

"You have no cause or reason to," Queen Elizabeth said.

The Archbishop of York said to Queen Elizabeth, "My gracious lady, go, and there carry your treasure and your goods. As for my part, I'll resign unto your grace the Great Seal of England King Edward IV gave to me to keep safe."

By giving the Great Seal to Queen Elizabeth, the Archbishop of York was taking her side. Legally, however, he was required to give the Great Seal to the new King Edward V.

The Archbishop of York continued, "May my fortunes be as good as the care I give to you and to all of your family! Come, I'll conduct you to the sanctuary."

CHAPTER 3

— 3.1 —

On a street in London stood the young Edward, Prince of Wales. With him were Richard, Buckingham, Cardinal Bourchier, Catesby, and others. Cardinal Bourchier was the Archbishop of Canterbury.

Buckingham said, "Welcome, sweet Prince, to London, your capitol."

Richard said, "Welcome, dear nephew, who is the sovereign of my thoughts. The weary way has made you melancholy."

"No, uncle," Prince Edward said, "but our crosses — vexations — on the way have made it tedious, wearisome, and heavy."

The crosses were the arrests of Rivers, Grey, and Vaughan.

Prince Edward continued, "I lack — and want — more uncles here to welcome me."

"Sweet Prince," Richard said, "the untainted and unsullied virtue of your young years has not yet dived into the world's deceit. You cannot distinguish more of a man than his outward appearance, which God knows seldom or never coincides with the man's heart. Those uncles whom you want were dangerous. Your grace attended to their sugared words, but you did not look on the poison of their hearts. May God keep you from them, and from such false friends!"

Rivers was the Prince's uncle; Grey was the Prince's step-brother; Vaughan was a family friend.

"May God keep me from false friends!" Prince Edward said. "But they were not false."

Richard saw some people coming, and he said, "My lord, the Mayor of London comes to greet you."

The Lord Mayor of London and his train of attendants came over to them.

The Lord Mayor said, "May God bless your grace with health and happy days!"

"I thank you, my good lord, and I thank you all," Prince Edward said. "I thought my mother, and my brother, the young Duke of York, would long before this have met us on the way. What a sluggard Hastings is, because he hasn't come to tell us whether they will come or not!"

Hastings arrived.

"And, in good time, here comes the sweating lord," Buckingham said.

"Welcome, my lord," Prince Edward said. Using the royal plural, he asked, "Will our mother come to meet us?"

"For what reason, God knows, not I," Hastings said, "your mother, the Queen, and your brother, the young Duke of York, have taken sanctuary. The young Duke of York would gladly have come with me to meet your grace, but his mother kept him by force."

"What a deceitful and perverse action is this of hers!" Buckingham said. "Lord Cardinal, will your grace persuade the Queen to send the young Duke of York to his Princely brother immediately? In case she denies this, Lord Hastings, go with him, and from her suspicious arms pluck him by force."

The Cardinal replied, "My Lord of Buckingham, if my weak oratory can from his mother win the young Duke of York, expect him here soon, but if she resists mild entreaties, then may God in Heaven forbid we should infringe the holy privilege of blessed sanctuary! Not for all this land would I be guilty of so deep a sin."

"You are too irrationally unyielding, my lord," Buckingham said. "You are too scrupulous over formalities and you are too traditional. Weigh this action against the grossness and unrefined character of this age, and you will find that you do not break sanctuary in seizing him. The benefit of sanctuary is always granted to those whose actions have deserved the place of sanctuary, and those who have the intelligence to claim it. This Prince, the young Duke of York, has neither claimed sanctuary nor deserved it, and so, in my opinion, he cannot have it. Therefore, in taking him from thence that is not there — a place of sanctuary where there is no sanctuary for him — you break no privilege or prerogative there. I have often heard of sanctuary men, but I have never heard of sanctuary children until now."

The Cardinal replied, "My lord, you shall overrule my mind for once."

He then said, "Come on, Lord Hastings, will you go with me?"

"I will go, my lord," Hastings replied.

Prince Edward said, "Good lords, do this quickly."

The Cardinal and Hastings exited.

Using the royal plural, Prince Edward said, "Say, uncle Richard, if our brother comes, where shall we stay until our coronation?"

"Where it seems best to your royal self," Richard replied. "If I may advise you, your highness should stay a day or two at the Tower of London. Then you can stay where you please, and where it shall be thought is most suitable for your best health and recreation."

"I do not like the Tower, of all places," Prince Edward said.

The Tower of London is where King Henry VI and Clarence had been killed.

Prince Edward asked, "Did Julius Caesar build that place, my lord?"

Buckingham answered, "He did, my gracious lord, begin that place; since that time, succeeding ages have re-built it."

According to tradition, Julius Caesar had built a fort on the location where the Tower of London was later built. William the Conqueror started building the Tower.

"Is it upon written record, or else reported orally successively from age to age, that he built it?" Prince Edward asked.

"Upon written record, my gracious lord," Buckingham replied.

"But if, my lord, it were not recorded in written documents, I still think that the truth would live from age to age, as if it were recounted orally to all posterity, even to the Day of Judgment."

Richard thought, *Those who are so wise when they are so young, people say, do never live long.*

"What do you say, my uncle?" Prince Edward asked.

Richard replied, "I say that without characters, fame lives long."

He thought, *Thus, like the formal Vice, Iniquity, I draw lessons from two meanings in one word.*

Richard was good with language. The word "characters" meant letters, as in written reports. Using that meaning, Richard was saying that fame could be long lasting even without written reports. Of course, the word "character" can refer to the collection of qualities that make a person a kind of person, such as a good person. Using that meaning, Richard was saying that evil people — people without good characters — could have long-lasting fame. King Richard III is well known today, hundreds of years after he died. Also, of course, people of good or innocent character can have long-lasting fame. Soon, the two young

Princes would be dead, but they would still have fame hundreds of years after their deaths.

The formal Vice, Iniquity, was a reference to the conventional Vice character in medieval morality plays. This character, which represented evil, was often named after a sin. The Vice often equivocated — used words that were ambiguous because they had more than one meaning.

"Julius Caesar was a famous man," Prince Edward said. "Actions that his valor did which enriched his wit, his wit set down to make his valor live. He was brave when he conquered Gaul, and his bravery increased his intelligence. With his intelligence he wrote the book *Commentarii de Bello Gallico* — *Commentaries on the Gallic Wars* — and so knowledge of his bravery lives on in fame. Death makes no conquest of this conqueror because now he lives in fame, though not in life.

"I'll tell you what, my kinsman Buckingham —"

"What, my gracious lord?" Buckingham asked.

"If I live until I become a man, I'll win our ancient right to France again, or die a soldier as I lived a King."

England and France had fought the Hundred Years' War because English Kings believed that they had a right to rule France.

Richard thought, *Short summers usually have a forward spring.*

Richard was alluding to, and changing, this proverb: Sharp frosts bite forward springs. The word "forward" meant "early" or "precocious." The word "springs" meant a certain season; it also meant "youth." One meaning of Richard's sentence was this: Those who die young are usually precocious.

The young Duke of York, Hastings, and the Cardinal arrived.

Buckingham said, "Now, at a good time, here comes the young Duke of York."

"Richard of York!" Prince Edward said. "How are you, our loving brother?"

"I am well, my dread lord," his brother replied. "I must call you 'my dread lord' now."

The word "dread" means "revered, held in awe, deeply honored."

"Yes, brother, you must call us that to our grief, as it is to yours," Prince Edward said, using the royal plural. "Just recently, the man — our father, King Edward IV — died who ought to have kept that title, which by his death has lost much majesty."

"How is our cousin, the noble Lord of York?" Richard asked.

"I thank you, noble uncle, for asking," the young Duke of York replied. "Oh, my lord, you said that worthless weeds are fast in growth. Prince Edward, my brother, has outgrown me by far."

"He has, my lord," Richard said.

"And is he therefore worthless?"

"Oh, my fair nephew, I must not say so."

"Then he is more beholden to you than I."

The young Duke of York meant that Prince Edward was beholden to Richard for not calling him a worthless weed. Earlier, Richard had not been so polite when talking to and about the young Duke of York.

"Prince Edward may command me as my sovereign," Richard said, "but you have power over me since you are a kinsman."

"Please, uncle, give me this dagger of yours."

"My dagger, little nephew?" Richard said. "With all my heart."

He thought, *With all my heart, I would like to give you this dagger in your heart.*

"Are you a beggar, brother?" Prince Edward asked.

"Yes, of my kind uncle, whom I know will give," the young Duke of York said. "And I begged for only a trifle, which will not hurt him to give away."

"A greater gift than that I'll willingly give my nephew," Richard said.

He thought, *I would like to give him the gift of Heaven, which I can do by having him killed.*

"A greater gift!" the young Duke of York said. "Oh, you must mean the sword that goes with this dagger."

"Yes, noble nephew, if the sword were light enough."

"Oh, then I see that you will part only with light, trivial gifts," the young Duke of York said. "In weightier things you'll tell a beggar no."

"The sword is too heavy for your grace to wear," Richard said.

"I would weigh it lightly, even if it were heavier," the young Duke of York said.

He was precocious, and he was punning. One meaning of what he had said was this: I would regard the gift lightly, even if it were heavier.

"Would you have my weapon, little lord?" Richard asked.

"I would, so that I might thank you as you call me."

"What do I call you?"

"Little."

The young Duke of York could be insulting; he was saying that he would little thank Richard for the gift.

Recognizing this, Prince Edward said, "My Lord of York will always be cross and perverse in his conversation. Uncle, you know how to bear with and endure him."

The young Duke of York said, "You mean, to bear me, not to bear with me. Uncle, my brother mocks both you and me. Because I am little, like a monkey, he thinks that you should bear me on your shoulders."

Trained bears sometimes carried monkeys on their backs. So did fools, aka jesters, and so the young Duke of York was calling Richard a fool. He was also saying that Richard's humped back was a good place for a monkey to sit.

The young Duke of York was good with language; he had made a triple pun: 1) "to bear with" meant "to put up with," 2) "to bear" meant "to endure," and 3) "bear" referred to the animal.

Buckingham said, "With what a quick and ready, sharply equipped wit he reasons! To mitigate the scorn he gives his uncle, he prettily and aptly taunts himself by likening himself to a monkey. To be so cunning at so young an age is wonderful."

Richard said to Prince Edward, "My lord, will it please you to continue on your way now? I and my good kinsman Buckingham will go to your mother to try to persuade her to meet you at the Tower of London and welcome you."

The young Duke of York said to his brother, "Will you go to the Tower, my lord?"

"Richard, my Lord Protector, will have it so," Prince Edward replied.

"I shall not sleep in peace at the Tower," the young Duke of York said.

"Why, what should you fear in the Tower?" Richard asked.

"My uncle Clarence's angry ghost. My grandmother told me he was murdered there."

"I fear no dead uncles," Prince Edward said.

"Nor none who live, I hope," Richard — Prince Edward's uncle — said.

"If they live, I hope I need not fear them. But come, my brother; with a heavy heart, thinking about my dead uncles, I go to the Tower."

Everyone exited except Richard, Buckingham, and Catesby.

"Don't you think, my lord," Buckingham said, "that this little prattling Duke of York was incited by his devious mother to taunt and scorn you thus opprobriously and insultingly?"

"No doubt, no doubt," Richard replied. "Oh, he is a perilous boy; he is bold, lively, ingenious, presumptuous, and intelligent. He completely takes after his mother, from the top of his head to his toe."

"Well, let them rest. We will not think about them for a while," Buckingham said. "Come here, Catesby. You have sworn as deeply to bring about what we intend as you have sworn closely to conceal the information we impart to you. You know our reasons for what we do. We told them to you as we were traveling together. What do you think? Will it be an easy matter to take Lord William Hastings into our confidence? Will he help us make the noble Richard, Duke of Gloucester, the King of this famous isle?"

Catesby replied, "Hastings so loves Prince Edward for the sake of his father, King Edward IV, that he will not be persuaded to do anything against Prince Edward."

Buckingham then asked, "What do you think, then, about Lord Stanley, Earl of Derby? Whose side will he take?"

"He will do exactly what Hastings will do."

"Well, then, I have no more to say but this," Buckingham said. "Go, noble Catesby, and subtly sound out Lord Hastings. See how he feels about our goal of making Richard King and summon him to go to the Tower of London tomorrow to attend a meeting about the coronation. If you find that he supports our goal, encourage him, and tell him all our reasons for wanting Richard to become King. If he is leaden, icy cold, and unwilling, then you be the same, too; and so break off your talk. Then give us notice of his inclination. Tomorrow we will hold two separate councils, wherein you yourself shall greatly be employed."

"Commend me to Lord William Hastings," Richard said. "Give him my greeting. And tell him, Catesby, that his ancient knot of dangerous adversaries — Rivers, Grey, and Vaughan — will be bled tomorrow at Pomfret Castle. Yes, they will be executed. And tell my friend, for joy of this good news, to give Mistress Shore one gentle kiss the more."

After King Edward IV had died, his mistress, Jane Shore, became Hastings' mistress.

"Good Catesby, go," Buckingham said. "Do this business well and soundly."

"My good lords, I will do this with all the care and attention I can," Catesby said.

"Shall we hear from you, Catesby, before we sleep?" Richard asked.

"You shall, my lord."

"Go to my house called Crosby Place," Richard said. "There you shall find us both."

Catesby exited.

"Now, my lord," Buckingham said, "what shall we do, if we perceive that Lord Hastings will not join our treacheries?"

"Chop off his head," Richard said. "We will decide something to do and then do it."

He added, "When I am King, you will be able to claim from me the Earldom of Hereford, and all the moveable possessions that my brother King Edward IV had there."

"I'll claim that promise when you become King," Buckingham said.

"And look to have it given to you very willingly," Richard said. "Come, let us eat early, so that afterwards we may digest — arrange and organize — our treacheries and put them in good order."

In front of Hastings' house, a messenger knocked at his door.

The messenger called, "My lord!"

From inside his house, Hastings called, "Who is knocking at my door?"

The messenger replied, "A messenger from the Lord Stanley."

Hastings opened the door and asked, "What time is it?"

"Four in the morning."

"Can't your master sleep during these tedious nights?"

"You will see that he cannot from what I have to say. First, he gives his greetings to your noble lordship."

"And then?"

"And then he sends you word that he dreamt this night that the boar had cut off his helmet and had obliterated the heraldic crest on the helmet. In other words, he dreamt that Richard, whose emblem is the boar, had cut off his head and had destroyed his family line. Besides, he says that two councils will be held, and that what may be determined at one of the councils may make you and him rue that you attend the other council. Therefore, he sent me to find out what your lordship will do. Will you immediately mount horses with him and as quickly as possible travel with him toward the north in order to shun the danger that his soul divines in his dream?"

Hastings replied, "Go, fellow, go, return to your Lord Stanley. Tell him not to fear the two separate councils. He and I will attend the one, and at the other will be my servant Catesby, and so nothing can occur that concerns Lord Stanley and me that I will not have knowledge of.

"Tell Lord Stanley that I say his fears are shallow and lack evidence. And as for his dreams, I wonder that he is so foolish to trust the mockery of unquiet slumbers. To flee from the boar before the boar pursues us would incense the boar to follow us although he had not intended to chase us.

"Go, tell your master to get up and come to me and we will both go together to the Tower of London, where he shall see that the boar will treat us kindly."

Hastings' words had an additional meaning that he did not intend. "The boar will treat us kindly" can mean that "the boar will treat us after its own kind, its own nature." In other words, it meant that Richard would treat them in accordance with his own wild nature — that of a dangerous boar.

The messenger replied, "My gracious lord, I'll tell him what you say."

The messenger exited, and Catesby arrived.

"Many good mornings to my noble lord!" Catesby said.

"Good morning, Catesby," Hastings replied. "You are up early and stirring. What is the news in this, our tottering state?"

"It is a reeling world, indeed, my lord," Catesby said, "and I believe it will never stand upright until Richard wears the garland of the realm."

"What? Wear the garland? Do you mean the crown?"

"Yes, my good lord."

"I'll have this crown of mine — the crown of my head — cut from my shoulders before I will see the crown of the King of England so foully misplaced," Hastings said. "But do you think that Richard is ambitious to become King?"

"Yes, on my life, and he hopes to find you an eager member of his faction who will work to get the crown for him. And thereupon he sends you this good news, that on this very same day your enemies, the kindred of the Queen, must die at Pomfret Castle."

The messenger was referring to the upcoming executions of Rivers, Grey, and Vaughan.

"Indeed, I am no mourner for that news because they have always been my enemies," Hastings said. "But, that I'll give my voice on Richard's side to help make him King, and to bar my master King Edward IV's truly descended heirs from becoming King, God knows I will not do it, even if I should die for my loyalty."

"May God keep your lordship in that gracious mind!" Catesby said.

"But I shall laugh at this a year from now," Hastings said. "I shall laugh because I live to look upon the tragedy of those who made my master — King Edward IV — hate me. I tell you, Catesby —"

"What, my lord?"

"Before I am older by a fortnight, I'll send some packing who do not yet think I will do so."

"It is a vile thing to die, my gracious lord, when men are unprepared and do not expect it," Catesby replied.

"Oh, it is monstrous, monstrous!" Hastings said, "And so it falls out with Rivers, Grey, and Vaughan, and so it will fall out with some other men, who think they are as safe as you and I, who, as you know, are dearly valued by Princely Richard and by Buckingham."

"Those two Princes both make high account of you," Catesby said.

He thought, *They account your head high upon the London Bridge.*

In this society, traitors and political enemies were beheaded, and the heads were displayed high at the end of poles on London Bridge.

"I know they do," Hastings replied, "and I have well deserved their high account of me."

Lord Stanley arrived.

Hastings said to him, "Come on, come on; where is your boar-spear, man? Do you fear the boar, and yet go about without a weapon to protect you?"

"My lord, good morning," Lord Stanley said. "Good morning, Catesby."

He said to Hastings, "You may continue to jest, but by the Holy Cross, I do not like the idea of these two separate councils."

"My lord, I regard my life as dear as you do yours," Hastings said, "and never in my life, I assure you, was it more precious to me than it is now. Do you think that unless I knew that we two were safe that I would be as triumphant as I am?"

"The lords at Pomfret Castle, when they rode from London, were jocular, and they supposed that they were surely safe, and they indeed had no reason to think otherwise, but yet you see how soon the day becomes overcast. This sudden stab of rancor by Richard against Queen Elizabeth's faction makes me suspicious. I pray to God that I prove to be needlessly cowardly! Shall we go to the Tower? The day is well begun."

"Come, come; let's go," Hastings said. "Do you know what, my lord? Today the lords you talk about — Rivers, Grey, and Vaughan — will be beheaded."

"They, for their loyalty, might better wear their heads than some who have accused them wear their hats," Lord Stanley said.

He meant that others deserved to be put to death more than Rivers, Grey, and Vaughan, who were loyal to King Edward IV and his family. The hats he referred to were hats that indicated official positions. Richard and Buckingham were both Dukes, and so they had the privilege of wearing the ducal hat in the presence of the King. No one below the rank of Duke was allowed to wear a hat in the presence of the King.

Lord Stanley said, "But come, my lord, let us go to the Tower."

A Pursuivant, a royal or state messenger who had the power to execute warrants, arrived.

Hastings replied, "Go on ahead of me while I talk with this good fellow."

Lord Stanley and Catesby departed.

"How now, sirrah!" Hastings said to the Pursuivant. "How goes the world with you? How are you?"

"Sirrah" was a word used to address someone of a lower rank or social status than the speaker.

The Pursuivant replied, "It is going better for me since your lordship is pleased to ask."

"I tell you, man, it is better with me now than when I met you last where we meet now. Then I was going as a prisoner to the Tower of London because of the false charges of the Queen's allies, but now, I tell you — keep it to yourself — this day those enemies will be put to death, and I am in a better state than ever I have been."

"May God preserve you, to your honor's good content and happiness!"

"Many thanks, fellow," Hastings said. He gave the Pursuivant some money and said, "There, drink that for me."

"May God save your lordship!" the Pursuivant said and then he departed.

A priest arrived and said to Hastings, "We are well met, my lord. I am glad to see your honor."

"I thank you, good Sir John, with all my heart," Hastings replied.

Priests were addressed as "sir" as a mark of respect.

"I am in your debt for your last sermon," Hastings said. "At the next Sabbath, I will pay my debt."

Hastings was speaking about giving money to the church, but God gave each of us our life, and so we owe God a debt. This debt can be paid back only with a death.

Hastings whispered in the priest's ear, most likely to tell him news of the upcoming executions of Rivers, Grey, and Vaughan.

Buckingham arrived and said to Hastings, "What, talking with a priest, Lord Chamberlain? Your friends at Pomfret Castle need the priest; your honor has no shriving work in hand. You do not need to confess your sins."

"Indeed, when I met this holy man, those men you talk about came into my mind," Hastings replied. "Are you going to the Tower of London?"

"I am, my lord; but I shall not stay long. I shall leave the Tower before your lordship does."

"That is likely enough, for I will wait to have dinner there."

Buckingham thought, *And supper, too, although you do not know it. You will be taken prisoner and executed, and so you will wait and wait for your supper, which will never be delivered to you.*

He said, "Come, will you go with me?"

"I'll go with your lordship," Hastings replied.

— 3.3 —

At Pomfret Castle, Sir Richard Ratcliff and some halberdiers led Rivers, Grey, and Vaughan to the place of execution.

"Come, bring forth the prisoners," Ratcliff said.

Rivers said, "Sir Richard Ratcliff, let me tell you this: Today you shall see a citizen die for truth, for duty, and for loyalty."

"May God keep the Prince from all the pack of you!" Grey said to Ratcliff. "A knot you are of damned blood-suckers!"

Vaughan said, "You who continue to live shall cry with woe for this later."

"Hurry up," Ratcliff said. "The end of your lives has arrived."

Rivers said, "Oh, Pomfret, Pomfret! Oh, you bloody prison. You are fatal and ominous to noble peers! Within the guilty enclosure of your walls, King Richard II was here hacked to death. To bring more disgrace and disrepute to your dismal seat, we give you our guiltless and innocent blood to drink."

Grey said, "Now old Queen Margaret's curse has fallen upon our heads, for standing by when Richard, Duke of Gloucester, stabbed her son: Edward, the Prince of Wales."

Rivers said, "She cursed Hastings, then she cursed Buckingham, and then she cursed Richard."

Old Queen Margaret had not cursed Buckingham, but no doubt Rivers wished that she had.

Rivers continued, "Remember, God, to hear old Queen Margaret's prayers for them, as now you hear her prayers for us. But as for my sister — Queen Elizabeth — and her Princely sons, be satisfied, dear God, with our true and loyal blood, which, as You know, unjustly must be spilt. Keep Queen Elizabeth, Prince Edward, and the young Duke of York safe."

"Hurry," Ratcliff said. "The hour of your deaths has come."

Rivers said, "Come, Grey. Come, Vaughan. Let us all embrace and take our leave, until we meet in Heaven."

They hugged, and then they left with Ratcliff and the guards.

In the Tower of London, several people sat at a table and talked: Buckingham, Lord Stanley, Hastings, the Bishop of Ely, Ratcliff, Francis Lovel, and others. This council of lords was meeting to discuss plans for the coronation of Prince Edward, who would be crowned King Edward V. Ratcliff had been present for the execution of Rivers, Grey, and Vaughan at Pomfret Castle, but he had then ridden unbelievably quickly to London.

Hastings, who as Lord Chamberlain presided over the meeting, said, "Now, my lords, the reason why we are meeting is to come to a decision about the coronation. In God's name, speak: When shall be the royal day?"

"Are all things ready for that royal time?" Buckingham asked.

"They are," Lord Stanley said, "and all we need to do is to name the day for the coronation."

"Let's have the coronation tomorrow, then," the Bishop of Ely said. "I judge that to be a suitable and happy day."

"Who knows what Richard, the Lord Protector, thinks about the coronation?" Buckingham asked. "Who is the most intimate friend of the royal Duke of Gloucester?"

"We think that you, yourself, your grace, is the most likely to know what he thinks," the Bishop of Ely replied.

"Who, I, my lord?" Buckingham said. "Richard and I know each other's faces, but as for our hearts, he knows no more of mine than I do of yours. And I know no more of his than you know of mine."

He then said, "Lord Hastings, you and he have a close friendship."

"I thank Richard's grace," Hastings said. "I know he much respects me. But, as for his opinion about the coronation, I have not asked him, nor has he delivered his gracious opinion to me in any way. But you, my noble lords, may name the day, and on behalf of the Duke of Gloucester I'll cast my vote, which, I presume, he'll take well and without offense."

Richard entered the room.

The Bishop of Ely said, "Now, at exactly the right time, here comes the Duke of Gloucester himself."

"My noble lords and all my kinsmen, good morning," Richard said. "I have been long a sleeper, but I hope that my absence has not caused you to neglect great matters that with my presence might have been dealt with and concluded."

"Had you not come upon your cue, my lord," Buckingham said, "Lord Hastings had pronounced your part — I mean, your vote — for the day on which to crown the new King."

"No man might be bolder than my Lord Hastings," Richard said. "His lordship knows me well, and he well respects me."

"I thank your grace," Hastings said.

"My lord of Ely," Richard said, "when I was last in Holborn, where you have your palace, I saw good strawberries in your garden there. I ask you to please send for some of them."

"I will, my lord, with all my heart," the Bishop of Ely said as he exited.

In this culture, strawberries were associated with danger and death. Strawberry bushes grow low to the ground and provide cover for dangerous snakes.

"My kinsman Buckingham, may I have a word with you?" Richard asked.

They went a short distance away from the other people present, and Richard said, "Catesby has sounded Hastings about our business of making me King, and Catesby finds the testy gentleman so hot, angry, and passionate that Hastings says he will lose his head before he shall give consent that the son of his master, King Edward IV, as he worshipfully calls him, shall lose the royalty of England's throne. He wants Prince Edward, King's Edward IV's son, to be crowned King Edward V."

"Go into another room, my lord," Buckingham advised. "I'll go with you."

Richard led the way out of the room; Buckingham followed him.

Lord Stanley said, "We have not yet decided on the day of triumph on which the Prince shall be crowned. Tomorrow, in my opinion, is too soon and sudden because I myself am not so well prepared as I would be if the day were postponed."

The Bishop of Ely returned and asked, "Where is the Lord Protector? I have sent for the strawberries."

Hastings said about Richard, "His grace looks cheerful and affable today. There's some idea or other that he likes well when he says to others, 'Good morning,' with such a spirit. I think there has never been a man in the Christian nations who can less hide his friendship or his hatred than he, for by looking at his face you immediately shall know what is in his heart."

Lord Stanley asked, "What of his heart have you perceived in his face by any liveliness he has shown today?"

Hastings replied, "I have perceived that he is offended by no man here, for if he were offended, he would have shown it in his looks."

"I pray God that Richard is not offended by anyone, I say," Lord Stanley replied.

Richard and Buckingham reentered the room. Anyone looking at Richard would think that he was angry.

Richard said, "All of you, please tell me what they deserve who conspire to bring about my death with devilish plots of damned witchcraft, and who have prevailed upon my body with their Hellish charms?"

Hastings replied, "The tender love I bear your grace, my lord, makes me most forward in this noble presence to doom the offenders, whoever they are. I say, my lord, that they have deserved death."

"Then let your eyes be the witness of this ill," Richard said, holding out his arm, which had been crippled since his birth. "See how I am bewitched. Look at how my arm is all withered up like a sapling blasted by lightning! Who are responsible for this? King Edward IV's wife, that monstrous witch, has joined with that harlot and strumpet Jane Shore, and by their witchcraft they have thus hurt me."

Richard was accusing Queen Elizabeth and Jane Shore, who had been King Edward IV's mistress and who was now Hastings' mistress, of being witches who had withered his arm.

"If they have done this thing, my gracious lord —" Hastings began.

"If —?" Richard interrupted "You protector of this damned strumpet — your mistress — you talk to me about 'ifs'? You are a traitor!"

Richard then ordered, "Off with his head! Now, by Saint Paul I swear that I will not dine until I see his cut-off head. Francis Lovel and Ratcliff, see that it is done. The rest of you, who love and respect me, rise and follow me."

Everyone exited except Hastings, Ratcliff, and Francis Lovel.

"Woe, woe for England!" Hastings said. "But not a bit of mourning for me because I, who have been very foolish, might have prevented this. Lord Stanley dreamt that the boar cut off his helmet, but I did not believe it, and I scorned the dream and distained to flee. Three times today my horse, which wore a finely decorated covering on its back and sides, stumbled and started when it looked upon the Tower of London as if my horse were loath to carry me to the slaughterhouse.

"Oh, now I need the priest who spoke earlier to me. I now repent that in front of the Pursuivant I exulted too much at how my enemies bloodily were butchered at Pomfret Castle. I thought that I was safe because I had Richard's grace and favor.

"Oh, Margaret, Margaret, now your heavy curse has lighted on poor Hastings' wretched head!"

"Hurry, my lord," Ratcliff said. "Richard, the Duke of Gloucester, wants to eat his dinner, but he won't until he sees that you are decapitated. Make a short confession of your sins; he longs to see your head."

"Oh, the momentary and temporary grace of mortal men, which we hunt for more than we do the permanent grace of God!" Hastings said. "Whoever builds his hopes on air, based on the favorable looks and opinions of mortal men such as Richard, lives like a drunken sailor on a mast, ready, with every sleepy nod, to tumble down into the fatal bowels of the deep."

"Come, come, hurry," Francis Lovel said. "It is useless to exclaim and complain."

"Oh, bloodthirsty Richard! Miserable England!" Hastings said. "I prophesy the most fearful time to you that any wretched age has ever looked upon.

"Come, lead me to the executioner's chopping block. Take to Richard my head. They who smile at me now shall shortly be dead."

Hastings had been executed illegally, without recourse to law. Now Richard had to provide an excuse for Hastings' death. He decided to pretend that a plot had broken out in the Tower of London and that Hastings had attempted to murder Buckingham and him. He and Buckingham had put on rusty, ugly armor as if they had been suddenly attacked and had been forced to put on whatever armor they could find. Now they were standing by a drawbridge of the Tower of London.

Richard said to Buckingham, "Kinsman, can you shudder, and change your color, murder — that is, stop — your breath in the middle of a word, and then begin again, and stop again, as if you were distraught and mad with terror?"

"Tut, I can imitate the deep tragedian, the actor who plays in tragedies," Buckingham said. "I can speak and look back over my shoulder, and peer on every side, tremble and startle at the mere wagging of a straw, all while pretending to be deeply suspicious. Ghastly looks are at my service, like forced smiles, and both are ready to do their duty at any time, to advance my stratagems.

"But has Catesby gone?"

"He has," Richard said. "Look, he is returning, and he is bringing the Lord Mayor of London with him."

The Lord Mayor and Catesby walked over to Richard and Buckingham, who quickly began acting.

"Lord Mayor —" Buckingham began.

Richard shouted, "Look to the drawbridge there!"

"Listen!" Buckingham said. "A drum!"

"Catesby, look over the walls," Richard ordered.

Catesby went to the wall to keep a "lookout."

"Lord Mayor, the reason we have sent —" Buckingham began again.

"Look behind you! Defend yourself! Here are enemies!" shouted Richard, who saw Ratcliff and Francis Lovel coming toward them.

"May God and our innocence defend and guard us!" Buckingham said.

"Be calm," Richard said. "They are our friends Ratcliff and Francis Lovel."

Ratcliff and Francis Lovel had with them Hastings' head.

Francis Lovel said, "Here is the head of that ignoble traitor, the dangerous and unsuspected Hastings."

"So dearly I loved the man," Richard said, "that I must weep. I took him to be the most plain and harmless creature who ever breathed upon this Earth a Christian. I made him my diary in which my soul recorded the history of all her secret thoughts. So smoothly he covered his vice with a show of virtue, that, with the exception of his obvious and open guilt — I mean his sexual intercourse with Shore's wife — he lived free from any hint of suspicion."

Buckingham said, "Well, well, he was the most secretive and hidden traitor who ever lived."

He said to the Lord Mayor, "If it were not for the great preservation and protection given to us by Heaven, we would not be alive to talk to you. Would you imagine, or almost believe, that this secret traitor had plotted to murder me and my good Lord of Gloucester today in the Council House?"

"Did he do that?" the Lord Mayor asked.

"Do you think that we are Turks or infidels who do not respect the rule of law?" Richard asked. "Do you think that we would, against the rule of law, proceed thus rashly to the villain's death unless the extreme peril of the case, the peace of England, and our personal safety forced us to do this execution of the traitor?"

"Now, may fair fortune befall you!" the Lord Mayor said. "He deserved his death, and you, my good lords, both have done the right thing, thereby warning false traitors not to attempt what this man, Hastings, has attempted. I never looked for anything better from him, after he once fell in with Mistress Shore."

"We had not decided that he should die yet," Richard replied. "We wanted your lordship to come and see his death. But the loving haste of these our friends, Ratcliff and Francis Lovel, somewhat against what we had intended, have prevented that because they quickly executed the traitor out of regard for our safety.

"My lord, we wish that you had heard the traitor speak, and timorously confess the manner and the purpose of his treason. That way you might well have told what you witnessed to the citizens, who perhaps may misunderstand us and bewail the traitor's death."

"But, my good lord, your grace's word shall serve as well as if I had seen him and heard him speak," the Lord Mayor said. "I believe what you have told me.

Do not doubt, both you right noble Princes, but that I'll acquaint our duteous citizens with all your just proceedings in this cause. I will tell them that you are fully justified in what you have done."

"That is why we wanted your lordship to be here to witness the execution of the traitor," Richard said. "We wanted to avoid the carping censures and criticisms of the world."

"But since you came too late to do what we intended," Buckingham said, "you can still witness — and serve as witness to — what you hear we intended, and so, my good Lord Mayor, we bid you farewell."

The Lord Mayor exited to address the citizens of London.

"Go, after him, kinsman Buckingham," Richard said. "The Lord Mayor hurries as quickly as he can towards Guildhall, the town hall of London. There, at the most suitable time, imply that King Edward IV's children are bastards, that they are not his and so are not eligible to succeed him as King. Tell them how King Edward IV put to death a citizen because the citizen said that he would make his son heir to the Crown, although the citizen meant only that his son would inherit his house, which was named the Crown, as a sign outside the house attested. That King Edward IV would do that is evidence that he feared that he was a cuckold. It is also evidence that he acted tyrannically over minor things. In addition, I want you to talk about his hateful lechery and his bestial appetite that required frequent change of the women with whom he slept. Say that his lechery was so vast that it stretched to their servants, daughters, and wives because his lustful eye and savage heart had no control over what they wished to make their prey.

"Indeed, if necessary, you may thus far come near my person: Tell them that when my mother was pregnant with that insatiable Edward, my Princely father, the Duke of York, then had gone to the war in France, and say that a just computation of the time shows that the child — Edward IV — was not fathered by him, as could be seen in Edward's appearance because he did not look anything like the noble Duke my father. But touch on this lightly, and subtly, because you know, my lord, my mother is still alive."

"Fear not, my lord," Buckingham said. "I'll orate as if the golden fee — the crown — for which I plead were for myself, and so, my lord, adieu."

"If you thrive well, bring the citizens to Baynard's Castle, one of my residences, where you shall find me well accompanied by reverend fathers and well-educated bishops."

"I leave now," Buckingham said. "Around three or four o'clock look for news from the Guildhall."

He departed.

Gloucester ordered, "Go, Francis Lovel, as quickly as you can to Doctor Shaw."

He ordered Catsby, "You go to Friar Penker."

He said to both of them, "Tell them both to meet me within this hour at Baynard's Castle."

Doctor Shaw was a Doctor of Divinity. Both Doctor Shaw and Friar Penker supported Richard.

Everyone exited except Richard, who said to himself, "Now I will go in to give a secret order to draw the brats of Clarence out of sight, and to give notice that no person, no matter how important, at any time shall have means of access to the Princes: Edward, the Prince of Wales, and his brother, the young Duke of York."

— 3.6 —

A Scrivener, a person who copies documents, looked at a legal document he was holding in his hands.

The Scrivener said to himself about the document he was holding, "This is the document containing the charges against and explaining why the good Lord Hastings was executed. This document is fairly written out in the correct style of handwriting and in the proper legal form, so that it may this day be proclaimed in Paul's Cross outside Saint Paul's Cathedral. And notice how well the succeeding events hang together. I spent eleven hours writing this document, for last night Catesby brought the original draft to me. The original draft itself took eleven hours to write, and yet within the past five hours Lord Hastings was still alive, untainted by accusation, unexamined in a law court, and free and at liberty.

"Here's a good world we live in! Here's a fine state of affairs! Why, who's so stupid that he does not see through this obvious fraud? Yet who's so blind, but he says that he does not see it? Everyone is afraid to speak up about what they know is true.

"Bad is the world, and all will come to evil when such bad dealings must be seen only in thought. Bad things happen when people cannot speak out against such evil."

At Baynard's Castle, Richard and Buckingham met.

Richard said, "What is the news, my lord? What do the citizens say?"

"Now, by the holy mother of our Lord, the citizens are completely quiet and do not speak a word."

"Did you say that Edward's children are bastards?"

"I did," Buckingham replied. "I talked about his contract to marry Lady Lucy, and about his contract by deputy to marry Lady Bona, sister-in-law to the King of France."

Edward IV had been engaged to marry Lady Lucy, with whom he had a child. Also, he had sent the Earl of Warwick to France to negotiate a marriage for him with Lady Bona, but he had changed his mind and married Elizabeth Grey, the widow of Sir John Grey. By this marriage, she became Queen Elizabeth. Richard had wanted these two previous contracts of marriage to be brought up because he hoped that the English subjects might regard them as invalidating King Edward IV's marriage to Queen Elizabeth. If that were to happen, then Richard would be regarded as the heir to the throne.

Buckingham continued, "I brought up the insatiable greediness of his sexual desires, and his rapes of the city wives, his tyrannous behavior wrought by trifling causes, and his own bastardy. I said that he was begotten when your father was in France. I said that he did not resemble the Duke of York, who was supposed to be his father. I also said that your appearance was an exact replica of your father and that you resembled him both in your form and in the nobleness of your mind. I talked about all your victories in Scotland, your discipline in war, your wisdom in peace, and your generosity, virtue, and fair humility.

"Indeed, I left out nothing that would help to show that you are fit to be the King of England. I emphasized all of your good points, and when my oratory grew to an end I asked everyone who loves their country's good to cry, 'God save Richard, England's royal King!'"

"Ah! And did they do that?" Richard asked.

"No, so God help me, they spoke not a word," Buckingham replied. "Instead, like dumb statues or breathing stones, they gazed at each other, and looked deadly pale. When I saw that, I reprehended them, and I asked the Lord Mayor what this willful silence meant."

"His answer was that the people were not accustomed to be spoken to by anyone except the Recorder. Then the Recorder was urged to tell my tale again by saying, 'Thus says the Duke' and 'Thus has the Duke inferred,' but to say nothing on his own authority.

"When he had done, some of my followers at the lower end of the hall hurled their caps into the air, and around ten voices cried, 'God save King Richard!'

"I took advantage of those few voices, and said, 'Thanks, gentle citizens and friends. This general applause and loving shout argue your intelligence and your love and respect for Richard.' At that time, I stopped speaking and came here."

"What tongueless blockheads they were!" Richard said. "Wouldn't they speak?"

"No, indeed, they would not, my lord."

"Won't the Lord Mayor and his brethren come here?"

"The Lord Mayor is here at hand," Buckingham replied. "Pretend that you are afraid that the citizens will hate you because of the execution of Hastings. Do not speak to them until they insistently petition you to speak to them. Get yourself a prayer book to hold in your hand, and stand in between two churchmen, my good lord, for on that ground I'll build a holy harmony and make you appear to be very religious.

"And do not be easily won to our request that you accept the crown. Play the part of a maiden: Always answer no, but eventually take it. Be like a virgin who says no but really means yes."

"I go now," Richard said, "and if you plead as well for them as I can say no to you for myself, no doubt we'll bring it to a happy issue. I will be convincing when I say no to accepting the crown; if you can be as convincing when you urge me to accept the crown, it will end up on my head."

"Go, go inside and upstairs," Buckingham said. "The Lord Mayor is knocking on the door of the courtyard."

Richard exited.

The Lord Mayor and some London citizens entered, and Buckingham said, "Welcome, my lord. I have been waiting for a while. I have been left to kick my heels while waiting to speak to Richard — I am dancing attendance on him. I am afraid that the Duke of Gloucester will not speak with anyone here."

Catesby entered the room, and Buckingham said, "Here comes his servant. What is the news, Catesby? What does Richard say?"

"My lord, he entreats your grace to visit him tomorrow or the day after. He is inside with two right reverend fathers, divinely bent to meditation, and he will allow no worldly suit to draw him away from his holy exercise and spiritual devotions."

"Return, good Catesby, to your lord again," Buckingham replied. "Tell him that I myself, the Lord Mayor, and the aldermen have come to have some conversation with his grace about deep designs and matters of great moment concerning no less than our general good."

"I'll tell him what you say, my lord," Catesby said, and then he exited.

"Ah, ha, my lord," Buckingham said to the Lord Mayor. "This Prince is not an Edward! Richard is nothing like his lecherous brother! He is not lolling on a lewd daybed, but instead he is on his knees and saying his prayers. He is not dallying with a pair of prostitutes, but instead he is meditating with two deeply learned divines. He is not sleeping, to fatten his idle body, but instead he is praying, to enrich his wakeful and vigilant soul.

"England would be happy if this gracious Prince were to take on himself the sovereignty thereof and become its King. But indeed I fear that we shall never convince him to become King."

"May God forbid that his grace should say no to our request that he become King!" the Lord Mayor said.

"I am afraid that he will say no," Buckingham said.

Catesby returned.

Buckingham asked him, "What is the news, Catesby? What does your lord say?"

"My lord, he wonders for what purpose you have assembled such troops of citizens to speak with him. Because his grace was not previously told that you were coming to see him, my lord, he fears that you mean no good to him."

Buckingham replied, "I am sorry that my noble kinsman should suspect that I mean no good to him. By Heaven, I come in perfect love to him; return again to Richard and tell his grace what I have said."

Catesby exited.

Buckingham said, "When holy and devout religious men are saying prayers with their rosary beads, it is hard to draw them away, so sweet is zealous contemplation."

Richard appeared on a balcony above them. He stood in between two Bishops. Catesby also stood on the balcony.

The Lord Mayor said, "Look! Richard is standing between two clergymen!"

Buckingham said to the Lord Mayor, "The clergymen are two props of virtue for a Christian Prince; they keep him from falling into sin because of vanity. Look! Richard is holding a book of prayer in his hand. The clergymen and prayer book are true ornaments by which you can know that Richard is a holy man."

He then said to Richard, "Famous Plantagenet, most gracious Prince, lend favorable ears to our request, and pardon us the interruption of your religious devotion and very Christian zeal."

"My lord, there is no need for such an apology," Richard said. "I rather ask you to pardon me, who, earnest in the service of my God, neglect the visitation of my friends. But tell me now, what is your grace's pleasure?"

"Our pleasure, I hope, is that which pleases God above, and all good men of this ungoverned isle," Buckingham said.

He called the isle ungoverned because it currently had no crowned King. Edward, Prince of Wales, who had become King Edward V with his father's death, had not been crowned.

Richard replied, "I suspect I have done some offence that seems ungracious in the city's eyes, and that you have come here to criticize my ignorance."

"You have committed an offense, my lord," Buckingham said. "I wish that it might please your grace, at our entreaties, to amend that fault!"

"Why else would I breathe in a Christian land?" Richard said.

"Then know that it is your fault that you resign the supreme seat, the majestic throne, the sceptered office of your ancestors, your state of fortune and position of greatness and your due of birth, the lineal glory of your royal house, to the corruption of a blemished stock. As long as you continue the mildness of your sleepy and contemplative thoughts, which here we awaken for the good of our country, this noble isle will lack her proper limbs. Her face is defaced with the scars of infamy; her royal stock has been grafted with ignoble plants and has almost been shouldered in the swallowing gulf of blind forgetfulness and dark oblivion. In short, because you are not wearing the crown, a lesser, undeserving person shall wear it.

"To right this wrong, we heartily solicit your gracious self to take on you the charge and Kingly government of this your land, not as Lord Protector, steward, substitute, or lowly agent for the gain of another person, but as the rightful successor by blood and inheritance. The throne belongs to you by your right of birth and your sovereignty; the throne is your own.

"For this reason, together with the citizens, who are your very worshipful and loving friends, and by their vehement instigation, in this just suit I have come to move your grace. We want you to be King of England."

Richard replied, "I don't know whether to depart in silence or to speak bitterly and rebuke you is best suitable for my social rank and for your social rank. If I don't answer you, you may perhaps think that I have tongue-tied ambition, which does not reply to you, but which has yielded to your request and has agreed to bear the golden yoke — the crown — of sovereignty, which foolishly you would here impose on me. But if I rebuke you for this entreaty of yours, which is so seasoned — made agreeable and given a palatable taste — by your faithful love to me, then, going to an extreme on the other side, I have criticized my friends.

"Therefore, to speak, and to avoid the first course of action, and then, in speaking, not to incur the last course of action, I answer you thus definitively and once and for all. Your respect for me deserves my thanks, but my lack of merit shuns your high request. I do not have the skills to be King of England.

"Even if all obstacles were cut away, and even if my path were clear and unobstructed to the crown, and even if the people regard the crown as being mine by law and by birthright, yet so much is my poverty of spirit, and so mighty and so many are my defects, that I prefer to hide myself away from my title to the throne. I am a ship that can survive no mighty sea, and I do not desire to be enveloped by my title to the throne and smothered in the vapor of my glory.

"But, thank God, there's no need for me to become King, and I would need much better qualities to help you, if you should need my help.

"The royal tree has left us royal fruit, which, mellowed by the passing hours of time, will well become the seat of majesty, and make us, no doubt, happy by his reign."

Richard was referring to Edward, Prince of Wales.

Richard continued, "I lay on him what you would lay on me, the right and fortune of his happy stars, which God forbid that I should wring from him!"

In his speech, Richard had mentioned his birthright, knowing the importance of hereditary succession. When he talked about Prince Edward, he mentioned "happy stars," or lucky astrological influence. Hearing this, Richard's audience would think that Richard had the better claim to the throne. And yet Richard could claim that he was saying that he did not want to take away his nephew's claim to be King of England.

Buckingham said, "My lord, this argues conscience in your grace, but the arguments you make are unimportant and trivial, if you carefully think about all the circumstances of this situation.

"You say that Prince Edward is your brother's son. We say the same thing, but we say that Prince Edward was not given birth to by King Edward IV's *wife*. King Edward IV was first contracted to marry Lady Lucy — your mother is a living witness to that vow — and afterward he used a deputy to get himself betrothed to Bona, sister to the King of France.

"These were both put off by a poor petitioner, Elizabeth Grey, a care-crazed mother of many children."

Elizabeth Grey had petitioned King Edward IV for the return of her late husband's lands and possessions.

Buckingham continued, "She was a beauty-waning and distressed widow, and she was in the afternoon of her best days. Elizabeth Grey captured King Edward IV's lustful eye. She seduced the greatest height of all his thoughts and led them to a base decline and loathed bigamy. She led him down and away from the greatness of his noble rank."

Because King Edward IV had married a widow, many people in his society regarded him as engaging in a bigamous "marriage," according to canon law. In addition, Buckingham was saying that Edward IV's pre-contracts of marriage to two other women made his marriage to Elizabeth Grey bigamous.

Buckingham continued, "By her, in his unlawful bed, he begot this Edward, whom we call the Prince of Wales because of etiquette. I could expostulate more bitterly, except that, to show respect to someone who is still alive, I put a limit to my tongue."

He was referring to the old Duchess of York, the mother of Edward IV and of Richard. Earlier, Richard had told him to hint that Edward IV was illegitimate.

Buckingham continued, "Then, my good lord, take to your royal self this proffered benefit of dignity. Accept the crown, if not to bless England and us, yet to draw forth your noble ancestry from the corruption of abusing times, and lead it to a lineal and truly derived course. Your lineage is true; do not allow a usurper to become King of England."

The Lord Mayer said, "Do become King, my good lord, your citizens beg you."

"Do not refuse, mighty lord, this love that is offered to you," Buckingham said.

"Oh, make them joyful — grant their lawful suit!" Catesby said.

"Alas, why would you heap these cares on me?" Richard replied. "I am unfit for state and majesty. I beg you not to take it amiss, but I cannot and I will not yield to you. I will not become King."

Buckingham said, "If you refuse to become King — as a result of your being, because of love and zeal, loath to depose the child, your brother's son, as we well know your tenderness of heart and kind, compassionate pity, which we have noted that you have shown to your kin, and equally indeed to all types of persons — yet whether you accept our suit or not, your brother's son shall never reign as our King. Instead, we are resolved to plant some other person in the throne to the disgrace and downfall of your house. And with this resolution we now leave you."

He then shouted, "Come, citizens! Damn! I'll beg no more that Richard become King!"

Richard said, "Oh, do not swear, my lord of Buckingham."

Buckingham and the citizens started to leave.

Catesby said to Richard, "Call them again, my lord, and accept their suit. Do, my good lord, lest all the land rue that you do not."

Richard replied, "Would you force me to go into a world of care? Well, call them again. I am not made of stone; your kind entreaties have penetrated my heart, albeit against my conscience and my soul."

Buckingham and the other citizens faced Richard.

Richard said, "Kinsman Buckingham, and you sage, grave men, since you will buckle fortune on my back and make me bear fortune's burden, whether I want to or not, I must have patience to endure the load, but if black scandal or foul-faced reproach follow, your forcing me to put on the crown shall acquit me from all the impure blots and stains thereof — I shall not be blamed because God knows, and you may in part see, how far I am from wanting to be King."

"God bless your grace!" the Lord Mayor said. "We see that you are reluctant to become King, and we will witness to others that this is so."

"In saying that I am reluctant to be King, you shall say only the truth," Richard said.

"Then I salute you with this Kingly title," Buckingham said. "Long live Richard, England's royal King!"

The Lord Mayor and the citizen said together, "Amen."

"Will it please you to be crowned tomorrow?" Buckingham asked.

"Whenever you please, since you insist that I be crowned," Richard replied.

"Tomorrow, then, we will attend your grace," Buckingham said, "and so most joyfully we take our leave of you."

Richard said to the two bishops, "Come, let us return to our holy task again."

He then said to Buckingham, "Farewell, good kinsman."

And he said to the departing Lord Mayor and citizens, "Farewell, gentle friends."

CHAPTER 4

— 4.1 —

A short distance from the Tower of London, two groups of people met. In one group were Queen Elizabeth, the old Duchess of York, and the Marquess of Dorset, one of Queen Elizabeth's sons. The other group included Lady Anne, who had married Richard, thereby becoming the Duchess of Gloucester. She was leading by the hand Lady Margaret Plantagenet, who was the young daughter of Clarence.

The old Duchess of York said, "Who are we meeting here? My granddaughter Plantagenet, led in the hand of her kind aunt of Gloucester?"

By marrying Richard, Lady Anne had become the aunt of Clarence's children.

The old Duchess of York continued, "Now, on my life, my granddaughter is wandering to the Tower of London, out of the love of her pure heart, to greet the young Princes."

She then said to Lady Anne, "Daughter-in-law, we are well met."

Lady Anne said to Queen Elizabeth and the old Duchess of York, "May God give both your graces a happy and a joyful time of day!"

"We wish you the same," Queen Elizabeth said. "Where are you going?"

"No farther than the Tower, and as I guess, we are on the same errand as you. We wish to greet the gentle, kind Princes there."

"Kind sister-in-law, thanks," Queen Elizabeth said. "We'll all go into the Tower together."

Sir Robert Brakenbury, Lieutenant of the Tower of London, walked over to them.

Queen Elizabeth said, "And, at a good time, the lieutenant is coming here."

She said to Brakenbury, "Master lieutenant, please, by your leave, tell us how my young son Prince Edward and my young son the Duke of York are doing?"

"Very well, dear madam," Brakenbury replied, "but by your leave, I may not allow you to visit them. The King has strictly ordered that you may not visit the Princes."

"The King!" Queen Elizabeth said. "Why, who's that?"

"I beg your pardon," Brakenbury said. "I meant the Lord Protector."

"May the Lord prevent Richard, the Lord Protector, from ever having the title of King!" Queen Elizabeth said. "Has he set a barrier between the Princes' love and me? I am the Princes' mother; who should keep me from them?"

"I am their father's mother," the old Duchess of York said. "I will see them."

"I am their aunt by marriage," Lady Anne said. "I love them as if I were their mother. Bring me to where I can see them; I'll bear your blame and take your duty from you at my own peril."

As the wife of Richard, the Lord Protector, Lady Anne believed that Brakenbury would allow her to see the Princes.

"No, madam, no. I may not put aside my duty," Brakenbury said. "I am bound to do my duty by oath, and therefore pardon me."

He departed.

Lord Stanley, Earl of Derby, walked over the group of women and said, "If I meet you, ladies, one hour from now, I'll salute your grace, the old Duchess of York, as the mother and honored beholder of two fair Queens."

One Queen, of course, was Queen Elizabeth. The Queen-to-be was Lady Anne.

He said to Lady Anne, "Come, madam, you must go immediately to Westminster Abbey. There you will be crowned Richard's royal Queen."

Queen Elizabeth said, "Oh, cut the lace of my bodice so that my closely confined heart may have some room to beat, or else I will faint because of this deadly, killing news!"

"These are despiteful tidings!" Lady Anne said. "This is unpleasant news!"

Dorset said, "Lady Anne, be of good cheer. Mother, how are you?"

"Oh, Dorset, do not speak to me!" Queen Elizabeth said. "For your own safety, leave this place! Death and destruction dog you at your heels; your mother's name is ominous to children. They will die because of who their mother is. If you want to outstrip death, go across the seas, and live with the Earl of Richmond, out of the reach of Hell — Richard and his government!

"Go, hurry, flee from this slaughterhouse, lest you increase the number of the dead, and make me die the slave of Margaret's curse, who said that I would not be a mother, a wife, or England's acknowledged Queen. As long as you remain alive, I am still a mother."

Lord Stanley said, "Your advice is full of wisdom and concern for your son, madam."

He said to Dorset, "Take swift advantage of all the hours. I will send a letter on your behalf from me to my stepson, the Earl of Richmond."

Margaret Beaumont had married Edmund Tudor, the first Earl of Richmond, and she had given birth to Henry Tudor, the second Earl of Richmond, who now lived in Brittany, France, and to whom Dorset would flee. Years after the first Earl of Richmond had died, Margaret Beaumont married Lord Stanley, Earl of Derby, and so he became the stepfather of Henry Tudor, the second Earl of Richmond.

Lord Stanley continued, "The letter shall tell my stepson to meet you on the way and welcome you. Be careful not to be captured by Richard's men because of unwise tardiness and delay."

The old Duchess of York said, "Oh, ill-dispersing wind of misery! Oh, my accursed womb, the bed of death! My womb has hatched a cockatrice and brought it into the world — the cockatrice murders everyone who does not avoid it."

Lord Stanley said to Lady Anne, "Come, madam, come with me to Westminster Abbey. I was sent to bring you there in all haste."

"And I in all unwillingness will go," Lady Anne said. "I wish to God that the inclusive verge of golden metal — the crown — that must go round my brow were red-hot steel, to sear me to the brain!"

Lady Anne was referring to a kind of torture in which a band of red-hot metal was placed around a traitor's forehead.

She continued, "Let me be anointed with deadly venom rather than holy oil as part of the ceremony of coronation, and let me die, before men can say, 'God save the Queen!'"

Queen Elizabeth said to her, "Go, go, poor soul. I do not envy your glory. My mood is such that I wish you no harm."

"No harm!" Lady Anne said. "Why? When Richard — he who is my husband now — came to me as I wept as I followed Henry's corpse, the blood was scarcely well washed from Richard's hands, blood that had come from my first husband — now an angel — and from that dead saint named King Henry VI.

"Oh, when I say I looked on Richard's face, this was my wish: 'Be you,' I said to him, 'cursed for making me, who am so young, so old a widow' — my grief over the death of my husband had aged me! I said to him, 'And, when you wed, let sorrow haunt your bed; and let your wife — if any be so mad as to marry you — be made as miserable by the life of you as you have made me miserable by the death of my dear husband!

"Even in so short a space as it would take me to repeat this curse, my woman's heart foolishly grew captive to his honey words and proved to be the subject of my own soul's curse, which ever since has kept my eyes from rest. I have never yet enjoyed the golden dew of sleep for even one hour in his bed; I have continually been awakened by his timorous dreams that frighten him. Besides, Richard hates me because of my father, the Earl of Warwick, and Richard will, no doubt, shortly be rid of me."

"Poor heart, adieu!" Queen Elizabeth said. "I pity you because of your troubles."

Lady Anne replied, "No more than from my soul I mourn for yours."

Queen Elizabeth said to her, "Farewell, you woeful welcomer of the glory of being Queen!"

"Adieu, poor soul, who take your leave of that glory!" Lady Anne replied.

The old Duchess of York said to Dorset, "Go to the Earl of Richmond, and may good fortune guide you!"

She said to Lady Anne, "Go to Richard, and may good angels guard you!"

She said to Queen Elizabeth, "Go to sanctuary, and may good thoughts possess you!"

She then said, "I will go to my grave, where peace and rest will lie with me! Eighty-odd years of sorrow have I seen, and for each hour I have felt joy I have endured a week of woe."

Queen Elizabeth said, "Wait and look back with me at the Tower. Pity, you ancient stones, those tender babes whom malice has enclosed within your walls! You are a rough cradle for such little pretty ones! You rough-hewn and ragged nurse, you old sullen playfellow for tender Princes, treat my babies well! And so foolish sorrow bids your stones farewell."

In the palace in London, the newly crowned King Richard III talked with Buckingham in the throne room. Catesby, a page, and others were present.

King Richard III ordered, "Move to the sides, everyone."

He then said, "My kinsman of Buckingham!"

Buckingham replied, "My gracious sovereign?"

"Give me your hand."

Holding onto Buckingham's hand for support, Richard III climbed up some stairs to the throne, saying, "Thus high, by your advice and your assistance, is King Richard III seated. But shall we wear these honors for only a day? Or shall they last, and we rejoice in them?"

"Always may they live and forever may they last!" Buckingham replied.

Richard III lowered his voice and began a private conversation with Buckingham, "Oh, Buckingham, now I play the role of a touchstone, to test you to see if you are indeed genuine gold."

A touchstone was used to test the purity of gold.

Richard III continued, "Young Edward, Prince of Wales, is still alive. Now guess what I am going to say."

"Tell me, my lord," Buckingham replied.

"Why, Buckingham, I say that I want to be King."

"Why, so you are, my thrice-renowned liege."

"Ha! Am I King? So I am, but Edward, Prince of Wales, still lives."

"True, noble Prince," Buckingham said.

"That Edward should continue to live has a consequence bitter to me: He will continue to be the 'true and noble Prince'! Kinsman, you have not been accustomed to be so dull. Shall I speak plainly? I wish the two bastards in the Tower of London dead, and I want them to be quickly dead. What do you say? Speak quickly; be brief."

"Your grace may do whatever you please."

"Tut, tut, you are all ice; your kindness freezes," Richard III said. "Tell me, do I have your consent that they shall die?"

"Give me some breathing time, some little time to think, my lord, before I answer your question. I will give your grace my answer soon."

Buckingham exited.

Catesby said quietly to a bystander, "The King is angry. See, he bites his lip."

Richard III said, "I will converse with iron-witted stupid fools and heedless boys. I want no one who looks at me with thoughtful eyes. High-reaching, ambitious Buckingham grows circumspect: He is wary, and he is unwilling to be a risk-taker."

He then called, "Boy!"

The page replied, "My lord?"

"Do you know anyone whom corrupting gold would tempt to perform a secret deed of death?"

"My lord, I know a discontented gentleman, whose humble means do not match his haughty mind," the page replied. "Gold is as good as twenty orators, and gold will, no doubt, tempt him to do anything."

"What is his name?"

"His name, my lord, is Tyrrel."

"I know the man a little," Richard III said. "Go, bring him here."

The page departed to perform his errand.

Richard III said to himself, "The deeply thinking and cunning Buckingham shall no longer be the neighbor to my counsels; I shall no longer tell him my plans. Has he, untired, for so long kept up with me, but now he must stop for breath?"

Lord Stanley, the Earl of Derby, entered the room.

"How are you now?" Richard III asked him. "What news do you bring with you?"

"My lord, I hear the Marquess of Dorset has fled to the Earl of Richmond in those parts beyond the sea where he lives."

The Marquess of Dorset was the son of Queen Elizabeth, aka Lady Grey, from a marriage previous to that with King Edward IV.

Having delivered his news, Lord Stanley stood to the side.

"Catesby!" Richard III called.

"My lord?" Catesby said.

"Spread abroad a rumor that Lady Anne, my wife, is sick and likely to die. I will give orders to keep her confined. Also, find me some meanly born gentleman, whom I will immediately marry to Clarence's daughter. Clarence's son is foolish, and I do not fear him."

Richard III was continuing to make plans to get rid of any rival claimants to the throne. He also wanted to get rid of Lady Anne so he could marry a woman who would give him a better claim to the throne of England than marriage to Lady Anne could.

Catesby was surprised by the orders and stood still.

Richard III was angry: "Look at how you are daydreaming! I say again, spread a rumor that Lady Anne, my wife, is sick and likely to die. Hop to it because it is very important that I stop all hopes whose growth may damage me."

Catesby departed to carry out his orders.

Richard III said to himself, "I must be married to my niece — my brother's daughter — or else my Kingdom stands on brittle glass. I must murder her brothers and then marry her!"

The niece whom Richard III wanted to marry was young Elizabeth of York, the daughter of King Edward IV and Queen Elizabeth.

He continued, "This is an uncertain way of gain — things can go wrong! But I have stepped so far in blood that sin will lead to sin. Tear-dropping pity does not dwell in this eye."

"This eye" was an evil eye.

The page returned, bringing with him Sir James Tyrrel.

Richard III asked, "Is your name Tyrrel?"

"I am James Tyrrel, and I am your most obedient subject."

"Are you, indeed?"

"Test me, my gracious sovereign."

"Do you dare to resolve to kill a friend of mine?"

"Yes, my lord, but I had rather kill two enemies."

"Why, there you have it," Richard III said. "I have two deep, deadly enemies, who are foes to my rest and who are my sweet sleep's disturbers. They are the two whom I want you to proceed against. Tyrrel, I mean those two bastards in the Tower of London."

"Let me have unobstructed access to them," Tyrrel said, "and soon I'll rid you of the fear of them."

"You sing sweet music," Richard III said. "Listen, come here, Tyrrel. Take this token; it will give you access to the two Princes."

Richard III handed Tyrrel a document.

He continued, "Rise, and listen to me."

He whispered to Tyrrel instructions about committing the murders, and then he said, "There is no more to say but this: Tell me that it is done, and I will love and respect you, and I will show you preferment, too."

"It shall be done, my gracious lord."

Using the royal plural, King Richard III said, "Shall we hear from you, Tyrrel, before we go to sleep?"

"You shall, my Lord."

Tyrrel exited.

Buckingham returned and said to Richard III, "My lord, I have considered in my mind the recent demand that you asked me about."

"Well, let that pass," Richard III replied, adding, "The Marquess of Dorset has fled to the Earl of Richmond."

"I have heard that news, my lord," Buckingham said.

Thinking to himself and addressing someone who was not present, Richard III said, "Lord Stanley, Earl of Derby, your wife's son is the Earl of Richmond, so you should be careful."

Buckingham said, "My lord, I claim your gift, my due by promise, for which your honor and your faith are pawned; I claim the gift of the Earldom of Hereford and the moveable property that you promised I should possess."

Still thinking to himself and addressing someone who was not present, Richard III said, "Lord Stanley, control your wife; if she conveys letters to the Earl of Richmond, you shall pay for it."

Buckingham said, "What does your highness say to my just demand?"

Still thinking to himself and ignoring Buckingham, Richard III said, "I remember that when the Earl of Richmond was a little silly boy, King Henry VI prophesied that he should become King. A King, perhaps, perhaps —"

"My lord!" Buckingham said.

Still thinking to himself and ignoring Buckingham, Richard III said, "How did it happen that the prophet — King Henry VI — could not at that time have told me, since I was nearby, that I should kill him?"

The word "him" was ambiguous. It could refer to King Henry VI or to the Earl of Richmond.

"My lord, your promise for the Earldom —" Buckingham began.

Still thinking to himself and ignoring Buckingham, Richard III said, "Richmond! When last I was at Exeter, the Mayor courteously showed me the castle, and he called it Rougemont. I was startled by that name because a bard of Ireland told me once that I should not live long after I saw the Earl of Richmond."

The words "Rougemont" and "Richmond" both mean "Red Hill."

Buckingham said, "My lord!"

Richard III replied, "Yes? What time is it?"

"I am so bold as to remind your grace of what you promised me," Buckingham said.

"Well, but what time is it?"

"Almost ten o'clock."

"Well, let the hour strike."

"Why let it strike?" Buckingham said.

Richard III replied, "Because, like a Jack, you keep the stroke between your begging and my meditative thinking. I am not in the giving mood today."

A Jack was a figurine of a man who struck the hour on clocks; a Jack was also an insulting term that meant a low-born man. Richard III was complaining that Buckingham's request to be given the Earldom of Hereford with all its moveable property was interfering with his thinking, and so Richard III wanted Buckingham to end his asking for the Earldom. After the Jack strikes the time, the Jack need strike no more. Richard III wanted Buckingham to quit making noise.

"Why, then let me know whether you will give me the Earldom or not."

"Tut, tut, you annoy me," King Richard III replied. "I am not in the giving mood."

Everyone except Buckingham left the room.

Buckingham said to himself, "Is this even real? He rewards my true service to him with such deep contempt! Did I make him King to be treated like this? Oh, let me remember what happened to Hastings, whom Richard III executed, and let me flee to Brecknock, my family's estate in southeast Wales, while my head, which is afraid, is still on my shoulders!"

<h1 style="text-align:center">— 4.3 —</h1>

Tyrrel entered King Richard III's throne room.

He said to himself, "The tyrannous and bloody deed is done. It is the most preeminent deed of piteous massacre that ever yet this land was guilty of. I bribed Dighton and Forrest, who are fleshed villains, bloody dogs, to do this ruthless piece of butchery. They are criminals who have killed before; they are dogs that have killed and have eaten a piece of the flesh of their kill. Yet they melted with tenderness and kind compassion, and they wept like two children while telling the sad stories of the deaths they had caused.

"'Like this,' said Dighton, demonstrating, 'those tender babes lay.'

"'Thus, thus,' said Forrest, also demonstrating, 'girdling one another within their innocent alabaster arms.'"

Alabaster was a white stone used in the creation of statues of humans in funerary monuments.

Tyrrel continued, "Forrest added, 'Their lips were four red roses on a stalk, which in their summer beauty kissed each other. A book of prayers lay on their pillow, which once almost changed my mind. But oh, the devil' — there the villain stopped. Dighton then said, 'We smothered the most perfect and sweet work of nature, that from the first, original, prime creation ever nature framed.'

"Thus both murderers are brought down by conscience and remorse. They could not speak any longer, and so I left them both in order to bring these tidings to the bloodthirsty King — and here he comes."

King Richard III entered the throne room.

Tyrrel said, "All hail, my sovereign liege!"

"Kind Tyrrel, will I be made happy by the news you bring?" Richard III asked.

The word "kind" has two meanings. It can mean "good and benevolent," and it can mean "a group of people who share similar character traits." Tyrrel and Richard III shared similar character traits.

"If news that I have done the thing you ordered me to do will make you happy, then you will be happy," Tyrrel replied. "For it is done, my lord."

"But did you see the two Princes dead?"

"I did, my lord."

"And buried, gentle Tyrrel?"

"The Chaplain of the Tower has buried them, but how or in what place I do not know."

"Come to me soon, Tyrrel, when I am enjoying dessert after the evening meal, and you shall tell me the story of the two Princes' deaths. In the meantime, think about how I may do you good. What you desire, you shall receive. Farewell until a short time from now."

Tyrrel departed.

Richard III said to himself, "The son of Clarence I have locked up in strict confinement. The daughter of Clarence I have basely married to an unimportant man. The sons of Edward IV sleep in Abraham's bosom — they are in Heaven. And Lady Anne, my wife, has bid the world good night."

Because Lady Anne, his wife, had died, Richard was in a position to marry someone who could strengthen his hold on the crown.

Richard continued saying to himself, "Now, because I know the Earl of Richmond, who is in exile in Brittany, France, aims to marry young Elizabeth of York, my brother Clarence's daughter, and, by that marriage-knot, he would look proudly over the crown because by uniting the House of York and the House of Lancaster, he would have a serious claim to the throne, to young Elizabeth of York I go as a jolly thriving wooer. I want to marry her before the Earl of Richmond does."

Young Elizabeth of York was, of course, a member of the House of York. The Earl of Richmond's mother, Lady Margaret Beaufort, was a great-granddaughter of John of Gaunt, Duke of Lancaster, who was the fourth son of Edward III. Such a marriage would end the conflict between the Yorkists and the Lancastrians, and if Henry Tudor, the second Earl of Richmond, became King Henry VII, he would become a Tudor King and could start a Tudor dynasty.

An excited Catesby entered the room and said, "My lord!"

"You come here so abruptly and without ceremony that you must be bearing important news," King Richard III said. "Is it good news or bad?"

"Bad news, my lord," Catesby replied. "The Bishop of Ely has fled to the Earl of Richmond, and Buckingham, backed with the hardy Welshmen, is in the field against you, and his army continually grows in size."

"The Bishop of Ely and the Earl of Richmond trouble me much more than the Duke of Buckingham and his hurriedly raised army," Richard III said. "Come, I have heard that timorous thinking is the indolent servant to dull delay. Delay leads impotent and snail-paced beggary. So then let fiery expedition and warlike enterprise be my wings. Let them be like Jove's messenger Mercury, and let them be heralds for a King! Come, muster the men. My counsel is my shield. We must act speedily when traitors brave the battlefield."

Standing in front of the palace, old Queen Margaret said to herself, "So, now prosperity begins to ripen, grow soft, and drop into the rotten mouth of death. I was prosperous, I matured, and soon I will die. The same is happening to my enemies. Here in these confines I have slyly lurked in order to watch the waning of my adversaries.

"I am witnessing the dire beginning of a tragedy, and I will go to France, hoping that what follows will prove to be as bitter, black, and tragic as the beginning."

Hearing a noise, she said to herself, "Withdraw out of the way and hide yourself, wretched Margaret. Who is coming here?"

Queen Elizabeth and the Duchess of York, wearing mourning clothes because of the deaths of the two Princes, walked onto the scene.

Queen Elizabeth was the widow of King Edward IV and the mother of the two Princes. The Duchess of York was King Richard III's mother and the grandmother of the two Princes; she was the widow of Richard, the third Duke of York, Richard III's father. In 1460, Richard, the third Duke of York, had died in the Battle of Wakefield.

"My young Princes!" Queen Elizabeth mourned. "My tender babes! My flowers with the buds unopened! My newly appearing sweets! If yet your gentle souls fly in the air and have not yet been judged and gone to Heaven, hover about me with your airy wings and hear your mother's lamentation!"

Old Queen Margaret said to herself, "Hover about her, and say that justice for the sake of justice has dimmed your infant morn to aged night."

Old Queen Margaret had suffered, and now Queen Elizabeth was suffering. Old Queen Margaret regarded this as just and rightful retribution — a just punishment for a crime against justice. Queen Elizabeth had aged due to grief, and old Queen Margaret also regarded that as just. She also regarded the deaths of the two Princes — they had gone quickly from the beginning to the end of their lives — as a just punishment for the deaths of her own loved ones.

The Duchess of York said, "So many miseries have cracked my voice that my woe-wearied tongue is mute and dumb. Edward Plantagenet, why are you dead?"

Edward Plantagenet was Edward, Prince of Wales, the older of the two Princes who had been murdered in the Tower of London.

Old Queen Margaret said, "Plantagenet does requite Plantagenet. Edward for Edward pays a dying debt."

Both Edwards were Princes of Wales. Old Queen Margaret had had her only son, Edward, with her husband, King Henry VI. This Edward had married Lady Anne. The other Edward was the older of the two Princes who had been murdered in the Tower of London. Old Queen Margaret believed that the only way the murder of her Edward could be requited or avenged was by the death of another person. That person turned out to be the older of the two Princes who had been murdered in the Tower of London.

Queen Elizabeth said, "Will you, God, flee from such gentle lambs as the two Princes, and throw them in the belly of the wolf? When have you ever slept when such a deed was done?"

Still talking to herself, Old Queen Margaret answered in place of God: "When holy Harry died, and my sweet son."

Holy Harry was Old Queen Margaret's husband, King Henry VI, and "my sweet son" was their son, Edward, Prince of Wales.

Regretting that she had lived long enough to experience the grief caused by the murders of the two Princes, the old Duchess of York sat and said, "Blind sight, dead life, poor mortal living ghost, woe's scene, world's shame, grave's due by life usurped, brief summary and record of tedious days, rest your unrest on England's lawful earth, unlawfully made drunk with the blood of the two innocent Princes!"

Queen Elizabeth sat by her and said, "Oh, that you — England's lawful earth — would as well give me a grave as you give me a melancholy seat! Then I would hide my bones in my grave, not rest them here. I wish that I were dead."

Old Queen Margaret revealed herself and said to them, "Who has any cause to mourn but I?"

She sat down by them.

She continued, "If ancient sorrow be most reverend, give my sorrow the benefit of seniority, and let my woes frown on the upper hand. If sorrow can admit society, count your woes again by viewing mine.

"I had an Edward, until a Richard killed him.

"My son, Edward, was killed by Richard, who is now Richard III.

"I had a Harry, until a Richard killed him.

"My Harry was my husband, King Henry VI, who was killed by Richard, who is now Richard III.

"You, Queen Elizabeth, had an Edward, until a Richard killed him.

"Your son Edward, Prince of Wales, was killed in the Tower of London, by Richard, who is now Richard III.

"You, Queen Elizabeth, had a Richard, until a Richard killed him.

"Your son Richard, the young Duke of York, was killed in the Tower of London, by Richard, who is now Richard III."

The old Duchess of York said to old Queen Margaret, "I had a Richard, too, and you killed him.

"You killed my husband, Richard, the third Duke of York, Richard III's father.

"I had a Rutland, too, and you helped to kill him.

"Rutland was one of my sons, and he was murdered just before my husband was murdered."

Old Queen Margaret replied to the old Duchess of York, "You had a Clarence, too, and Richard killed him. Richard, who is now Richard III, killed his brother Clarence in the Tower of London.

"From forth the kennel of your womb has crept a Hellhound that hunts us all to death. That Hellhound is Richard, who was born with teeth. That dog, which had his teeth before he had his eyes, since dogs are born blind, to bite lambs and lap their gentle blood, that foul defacer of God's handiwork, that killer of humans created in the image of God, that excellent grand tyrant of the earth, who reigns in the inflamed eyes of weeping souls — that is the creature your womb let loose to chase us to our graves.

"Oh, upright, just, and true-disposing God, how do I thank you that this carnal cur preys on the children who came from his mother's body, and makes her share a pew in church with other mourning mothers!"

The old Duchess of York said to old Queen Margaret, widow of King Henry VI, "Oh, Harry's wife, do not triumph in my woes! May God witness with me that I have wept for your woes."

"Bear with me," old Queen Margaret said. "I am hungry for revenge, and now I fill myself by beholding it.

"Your Edward is dead, who stabbed my Edward.

"Your son, King Edward IV, stabbed and helped kill my son: Edward, Prince of Wales.

"Your other Edward — the older of the two young Princes, died, to requite Edward, my son.

"Young Richard, Duke of York, the younger of the two Princes, is only a little something added to the revenge, because both your Edward IV and your Edward, Prince of Wales, together cannot match the loss of the high perfection of my Edward, Prince of Wales.

"Clarence, your son, is dead who helped kill Edward, Prince of Wales, my son.

"And the beholders of this tragedy that is the murder of my son by your Edward IV, Clarence, and Richard III are all untimely smothered in their dusky graves. Those beholders — bystanders — are the adulterer Hastings, and Rivers, Vaughan, and Grey.

"Richard III still lives. He is Hell's black agent, kept alive only to serve Hell by buying souls and sending them there. But at hand is his deplorable and unpitied end. Earth gapes, Hell burns, fiends roar, and saints pray to have Richard III die and suddenly be conveyed away from the Land of the Living. Cancel his bond of life, dear God, I pray, so that I may live to say, 'The dog is dead'!"

Queen Elizabeth said, "You prophesied that the time would come that I would wish for you to help me curse that bottle-bodied spider, that foul hunchbacked toad, that Richard!"

Old Queen Margaret said, "I called you then the worthless ornamentation of my fortune. I called you then a poor shadow and image, a painted — not real — Queen. I called you the mere semblance of what I was. I called you the flattering preface of a dreadful pageant.

"You are a person who has been heaved high on the Wheel of Fortune, only to be hurled down below.

"You are a mother who has been only mocked — not blessed — with two sweet babes who have so quickly been taken from you.

"You are only a dream of what you used to be; you are a breath, a bubble, an empty symbol of dignity, a garish flag that is the target of every dangerous soldier. You are a Queen only in jest, brought onto the scene only to be an extra.

"Where is your husband now?

"Where are your brothers?

"Where are your children?

"What makes you rejoice?

"Who pleads to you and cries, 'God save the Queen'?

"Where are the bowing peers who flattered you?

"Where are the thronging troops who followed you?

"Go through all this point by point, and see what now you are.

"Instead of being a happy wife, you are a very distressed widow.

"Instead of being a joyful mother, you are one who mourns the name.

"Instead of being a Queen, you are a very wretched creature who is crowned with care and worry.

"Instead of being a person to whom people plead, you are a person who humbly pleads.

"Instead of being a person who scorns me, you are now scorned by me.

"Instead of being a person who is feared by all, you now fear one person — Richard III.

"Instead of being a person who commands all, you are obeyed by none.

"Thus has the course of justice wheeled about, and it has left you a prey to time. Now if you think about what you have been, you are tortured all the more, because of what you are now.

"You usurped my position as Queen of England, and therefore don't you usurp the just and proper proportion of my sorrow? Now your proud neck bears half of my burdensome yoke, from which now and here I slip my weary neck, and leave the burden of it all on you.

"Farewell, York's wife, and farewell, Queen of sad mischance. These English woes will make me smile in France.

"Goodbye, old Duchess of York and Queen Elizabeth. I am going to France, where I shall enjoy your misery."

Queen Elizabeth pleaded, "You are well skilled in making curses. Stay awhile, and teach me how to curse my enemies!"

Old Queen Margaret replied, "Cease sleeping during the nights, and fast during the days. Compare the dead happiness of the past with the woe that lives today. Think that your babes were fairer and better than they were, and think that he who slew them is fouler than he is. Magnifying your loss makes the bad causer of your loss worse. Meditating on these things will teach you how to curse."

"My words are dull," Queen Elizabeth said. "Make my words lively like your words!"

"Your woes will make them sharp and make them pierce like mine," old Queen Margaret said, and then she exited.

The old Duchess of York asked, "Why should calamity be full of words?"

Queen Elizabeth replied, "Words are windy attorneys that plead the woes of their client, they are the heirs of joys that died without leaving a will to pass on good things, and they are poor breathing orators of miseries!

"Let words have scope. Although the content that they impart helps not at all, yet words do ease the grieving heart."

"If that is true, then do not be tongue-tied," the old Duchess of York said. "Go with me, and in the breath of bitter words let's smother my damned son, Richard III, who smothered your two sweet sons. I hear his army's drums. Let's be copious in our outcries."

King Richard III and his army entered the scene. The old Duchess of York and Queen Elizabeth stood in his way. Because they were wearing veils as part of their mourning clothing, Richard III did not recognize them.

He asked, "Who intercepts my setting out for war?"

His mother, the old Duchess of York, said, "I am she who might have intercepted you, by strangling you in her accursed womb, and kept you from committing all the slaughters, wretch, that you are responsible for!"

Queen Elizabeth asked, "Do you hide your forehead with a golden crown? On your forehead should be engraved, if justice prevailed, the slaughter of the true Prince who owned and possessed by right that crown, and the dire deaths of my two sons and brothers!

"Tell me, you villain slave, where are my children?"

The old Duchess of York asked, "You toad, where is your brother Clarence? And where is little Ned Plantagenet, his son?"

"Ned" is a nickname for "Edward." Edward was one of the two Princes whom Richard had ordered to be murdered.

Queen Elizabeth asked, "Where are kind Hastings, Rivers, Vaughan, and Grey?"

Queen Elizabeth had no reason to call Hastings kind except to magnify one of Richard's sins.

King Richard III called for martial music to drown out the cries of the two women: "A flourish, trumpets! Strike the call to battle, drums! Let not the Heavens hear these telltale, gabbling women rail against the Lord's anointed King. Play, I say!"

Military music filled the air, and Richard III said to his mother and sister-in-law, "Either be calm, and talk to me with respect, or with the clamorous noise of war I will thus drown out your exclamations."

"Are you my son?" the old Duchess of York asked.

"Yes, I thank God, my father, and yourself."

"Then patiently hear my impatience."

Richard III replied, "Madam, I have a touch of your temperament, which cannot endure the tone of reproof."

"Let me speak!" the old Duchess of York demanded.

"Speak, then, but I'll not listen to you."

"I will be mild and gentle in my speech."

"Also be brief, good mother, because I am in a hurry."

"Are you so hasty?" his mother asked. "I have waited for you, God knows, in anguish, pain, and agony. I gave birth to you."

"And didn't I come at last to comfort you?"

"No, you did not, by the Holy Cross. You well know that you came on Earth to make the Earth my Hell. Your birth was a grievous burden to me. In your infancy you were peevish and disobedient. Your schooldays were frightening, desperate, wild, and furious. Your time of prime of manhood was daring, bold, and venturous. Your time of maturity was proud, subdued, bloodthirsty, and treacherous; it was milder, but yet more harmful because you appeared to be kind when actually you felt hatred. What cheerful hour can you name that ever graced me in your company?"

"Indeed, I can name only one cheerful hour — Humphrey Hour," Richard replied. "He graced you in my company by calling you away from my company — he asked you to go and eat breakfast. If I am so disgracious and displeasing in your sight, then let me march on, and not offend your grace."

He then ordered, "Strike the drum."

The old Duchess of York said, "Please, hear me speak."

Richard III replied, "You speak too bitterly."

"Hear me speak briefly to you because I shall never speak to you again."

"Speak."

"Either you will die, by God's just ordinance, before you return as a conqueror from this war, or I with grief and extreme old age shall perish and never look upon your face again. Therefore take with you my most heavy and serious curse, which, on the day of battle, will tire you more than all the full and heavy suit of armor that you are wearing!

"My prayers will fight on the side of the party opposing you, and there the little souls of Edward IV's children — the two Princes — will whisper to the spirits of your enemies and promise them success and victory.

"Bloodthirsty you are, and bloody will be your end. Shame serves your life and does your death attend."

Having cursed her son, the old Duchess of York exited.

"Although I have far more cause, yet I have much less spirit to curse you," Queen Elizabeth said, "but I say 'amen' to everything that your mother said."

"Wait, madam," Richard III said. "I must speak with you."

"I have no more sons of the royal blood for you to murder," Queen Elizabeth said. "As for my daughters, Richard, they shall be praying nuns, not weeping Queens, and therefore you ought not to aim at them and take their lives."

"You have a daughter called young Elizabeth of York," Richard III said. "She is virtuous and fair, royal and gracious."

"And must she die for that? Oh, let her live, and I'll corrupt her manners and morals, stain her beauty, and slander myself by saying that I was false to Edward IV's bed and cheated on him. I will throw over her the veil of a bad and infamous reputation so she may live unscarred by bleeding slaughter. I will confess — falsely — that she is not Edward's daughter."

"Do not wrong her birth," Richard III said. "She is of royal blood."

"To save her life, I'll say she is not of royal blood."

"Her life is safest only if she is of royal blood," Richard III said.

He wanted to marry young Elizabeth of York in order to make his hold on the throne tighter; if she were not believed to be the legitimate daughter of King Edward IV, marrying her would not help him do that.

Queen Elizabeth said, "And only in that safety died her brothers."

Young Elizabeth of York's brothers — the two Princes — had died because they were the legitimate sons of King Edward IV.

"At their births, the good stars were hostile to them," Richard III said.

"No, bad family members were hostile to their lives."

"Entirely unavoidable is the doom of destiny," Richard III said.

"True, when avoided grace — you, Richard, lack the grace of God — makes destiny. My babes were destined to have a fairer death, a death without violence, if grace had blessed you with a fairer life, a life with fewer blemishes."

"You speak as if I had slain my nephews."

"They were your nephews, indeed, and by their uncle they were cheated of comfort, Kingdom, kindred, freedom, and life," Queen Elizabeth said. "No matter whose hand pierced their tender hearts, your head, all indirectly, gave the order. No doubt the murderous knife was dull and blunt until it was whetted on your stone-hard heart, to revel in the entrails of my lambs.

"Except that continual experience of grief makes wild grief tame, my tongue should to your ears not name my boys until my fingernails were anchored in your eyes, and I, in such a desperate bay of death, like a poor ship bereft of sails and tackling, would rush against you and be wrecked all to pieces on your rocky bosom."

Richard III said, "Madam, may I so thrive and prevail in my enterprise and dangerous success of bloody wars to the extent that I intend to do more good to you and yours than ever you or yours were by me wronged!"

"What good is covered by the face of Heaven that can yet be uncovered and do me good?"

"The advancement of your children, gentle lady," Richard III replied.

"Advancement up to some scaffold, there to lose their heads."

"No, advancement to the dignity and height of honor, the high imperial symbol of this Earth's glory."

"Flatter my sorrows by telling me about it," Queen Elizabeth said. "Tell me: What rank, what dignity, what honor can you give to any child of mine?"

"Everything I have; yes, I will endow a child of yours with myself and all I have as long as in the Lethe of your angry soul you drown the sad remembrance of those wrongs that you suppose I have done to you."

The Lethe was a river in the Land of the Dead that causes forgetfulness in the souls who drank from it. Richard III wanted Queen Elizabeth to forget the sins that he had committed against her and her family.

"Be brief, lest the report of your kindness last longer in the telling than in the duration of your kindness," Queen Elizabeth said.

Richard III lied, "Then know that from my soul I love your daughter."

Richard III had said that he loved her daughter with all his soul, but Queen Elizabeth deliberately misunderstood him to be saying that he loved her daughter apart from his soul — that is, not with his soul, and not at all.

"My daughter's mother thinks it with her soul," Queen Elizabeth said.

"What do you think?"

"That you love my daughter from your soul. So from your soul's love you loved her brothers; and from my heart's love I thank you for it."

"Don't be so hasty to misinterpret my meaning," Richard III said. "I mean that with my soul I love your daughter, and I mean to make her Queen of England."

"Tell me, who do you mean shall be her King?"

"He who makes her Queen. Who else should he be?"

"Do you mean yourself? You shall be her King?"

"I, yes, I. What do you think about it, madam?"

"How can you woo her?"

"How to woo her is something that I want to learn from you, as you are the one who is best acquainted with her temperament."

"And will you learn how to do that from me?"

"Madam, with all my heart," Richard III said.

"Then do what I tell you to do. Send to her, by the man who slew her brothers, a pair of bleeding hearts. On those hearts engrave the names Edward and York. Perhaps then she will weep. Therefore present to her — as once old Queen Margaret gave a handkerchief steeped in your brother Rutland's blood to your father — a blood-soaked handkerchief. Say to her that this handkerchief soaked up the red blood that drained from her sweet brothers' bodies and tell her to dry her weeping eyes with it. If this inducement does not force her to love you, send her a story of your noble acts. Tell her you killed her uncle Clarence. Tell her you killed her uncle Rivers. Yes, and tell her that for her sake you killed her good aunt Anne."

"Come, come, you mock me; this is not the way for me to win your daughter."

"There is no other way unless you could put on some other shape, and not be the Richard who has done all this."

"Say that I did all this because of love of her," Richard III said.

"Then indeed she cannot choose but hate you since you have bought love with such a bloody spoil."

"Look, what is done cannot be now undone," Richard said. "Men sometimes make mistakes, which later hours give leisure to repent. If I took the Kingdom from your sons, then to make amends I'll give the Kingdom to your daughter. If I have killed the children born from your womb, then to rejuvenate your offspring I will beget children with your daughter.

"A grandmother's name is little less in love than is the loving title of a mother. Grandchildren are like children, but they are one step below. Grandchildren are of your substance and your character and your blood. Children and grandchildren cause the same amount of effort and pain, save for a night of groans in childbirth that will be endured by her, young Elizabeth of York, for whom you have already endured a night of groans.

"Your children were a vexation to your youth, but mine shall be a comfort to your old age. The loss you have is only a son who was only briefly King — Edward V — and never crowned, and by that loss your daughter will be made Queen.

"I cannot make you what amends I would like to make, so therefore accept such kindness as I can give to you.

"This fair alliance between your daughter and me shall quickly call home Dorset, your son, who now with a frightened soul leads discontented steps in foreign soil, and his returning home will result in him getting high promotions and great dignity.

"I, the King, who will call your beauteous daughter wife, shall familiarly call your son Dorset brother.

"Again you shall be mother to a King — this time you shall be a mother-in-law to a King.

"And all the ruins of distressful times shall be repaired with double riches of content.

"We have many good days to see in the future. The liquid drops of tears that you have shed shall come again, transformed to orient pearls, advantaging their loan with interest of ten times double gain of happiness.

"Go, my mother-in-law to be, go to your daughter and make bold her bashful years with your experience. Prepare her ears to hear a wooer's tale that will put in her tender heart the aspiring flame of golden sovereignty. Acquaint the Princess with the sweet silent hours of marriage joys, and when this arm of mine has chastised and punished the petty rebel, dull-brained Buckingham, I will return wearing triumphant garlands, and I will lead your daughter to a conqueror's bed. To her I will tell about the conquest I have won, and she shall be the sole victress, the conqueror of Caesar — Caesar's Caesar."

"Who would it be best I say is wooing her?" Queen Elizabeth asked. "Shall I say her father's brother wants to be her husband? Or shall I say her wooer is her uncle? Or, he who slew her brothers and her uncles? What title shall I call you that God, the law, my honor, and her love can make seem pleasing to her young and tender years?"

"Say that fair England shall enjoy fair peace as a result of this alliance and marriage."

"Fair peace that England shall purchase with forever-lasting war."

"Say that the King, who may command, begs her to marry him."

"You beg her to do what the King of Kings forbids."

The church forbids marriage between uncle and niece.

"Say that she shall be a high and mighty Queen," Richard III said.

"That is a title that she shall bewail, as does her mother," Queen Elizabeth said.

"Say that I will love her everlastingly."

"But how long shall that 'everlastingly' last?"

"It shall remain sweetly in force until her fair life ends."

"But how long fairly shall her sweet life last?"

"As long as Heaven and nature lengthen it."

"As long as Hell and Richard want it to last."

"Say that I, her sovereign, am her subject love."

"But she, your subject, loathes such sovereignty."

"Be eloquent on my behalf when you speak to her," Richard III said.

"An honorable tale succeeds best when it is plainly told," Queen Elizabeth said.

"Then in plain terms tell her my loving tale."

"Plain and *not* honorable is too harsh a style," Queen Elizabeth said.

"Your arguments for going against my wishes are too shallow and too quick."

One meaning of "quick" is "alive," and Queen Elizabeth deliberately misunderstood Richard to use that meaning rather than "hasty."

"Oh, no, my arguments are too deep and dead," Queen Elizabeth said. "Too deep and dead are my poor infants in their grave."

"Harp not on that string, madam; that is past," Richard said.

"Harp on it I always shall until my heartstrings break."

"Now, by my George, my garter, and my crown —"

"You have profaned your George, dishonored your garter, and usurped your crown," Queen Elizabeth said.

The George is a jeweled ornament depicting Saint George. The garter is a decorative leg-band showing membership in the Order of the Garter, the highest order of English knighthood. Both the George and the garter are emblems of chivalry.

Richard III began to say, "I swear —"

"— by nothing," Queen Elizabeth interrupted, "because this is no oath. The George, profaned by you, has lost its holy honor. The garter, blemished by you, has pawned its knightly virtue. The crown, usurped by you, has disgraced its Kingly glory. If you want to swear by something that will make your oath be believed, swear by something that you have not wronged."

"Now, by the world —"

"The world is full of your foul wrongs."

"My father's death —"

"Your life has dishonored your father's death."

"Then, by myself —"

"You misuse yourself. You are not the person you ought to be."

"Why then, by God —"

"You have wronged God most of all," Queen Elizabeth said. "If you had feared to break the oath you made by Him, the unity between opposing factions that King Edward IV, your brother, made would not have been broken, nor had my brother — Anthony Woodville, Earl Rivers — been slain. If you had feared to break the oath you made by Him, the imperial metal, the crown that now circles your brow, would have graced the tender temples of my child, and both of the young Princes would still be breathing here in this world, but now they are two young playfellows to dust — your broken faith has made them a prey for worms.

"What can you swear by now?"

"The time to come," Richard III said.

"You have wronged the future, for I myself have many tears to wash my face in the future because of wrongs that you have committed in the past. Some children live, whose parents you have slaughtered, who will spend their youths without parental guidance, and they will wail for it in their old age. Some parents live, whose children you have butchered, parents who are now old, withered, barren plants, and in their old age they bewail the loss of their children.

"Swear not by the time that is to come; for that you have misused before it is used, by misusing time that has already passed."

"As I intend to prosper and repent, so may I thrive in my dangerous battle against hostile arms! May I destroy myself if I do not intend to prosper and repent! May Heaven and Lady Fortune keep happy hours away from me! Day, do not give me your light; night, do not give me your rest! Oppose me, all planets of good luck, and ruin my proceedings. May all this happen to me if I do not regard your beauteous Princessly daughter with the love of a pure heart, with immaculate devotion, and with holy thoughts. In her consists my happiness and yours. Unless I have her, what will follow to this land and me, and to you, herself, and many a Christian soul, will be death, desolation, ruin, and decay. These bad things cannot be avoided except by my marrying her. These bad things will not be avoided except by my marrying her.

"Therefore, good mother-in-law to be — I must call you so — be the attorney of my love to her. Plead what I will be, not what I have been. Do not plead what I deserve, but what I will deserve. Urge the necessity and the state of times, and do not be obstinately foolish when great affairs of the world are at stake."

"Shall I thus be tempted by the devil?" Queen Elizabeth asked.

"Yes, if the devil tempts you to do good," Richard III replied.

According to Christian belief, the devil tempts people to do good only when the result will be a greater evil.

"Shall I forget myself to be myself? Shall I forget that I was the mother of a King — Edward V — whom you killed? Shall I forget that simply so that I can be the mother of a Queen?"

"Yes, you should forget that memory if that memory hurts you."

"But you killed my children."

"But I will bury them in your daughter's womb, where in that nest of spicery they shall breed copies of themselves, to your consolation."

Richard III was referring to the myth of the phoenix, a bird that sets itself on fire in a nest of spices. After burning, the phoenix arises, newly young, from the ashes.

"Shall I go now and persuade my daughter to do what you want her to do?" Queen Elizabeth asked.

"Yes, and by doing so, you will be a happy mother."

"I am going now," Queen Elizabeth said. "Write to me very soon, and I will let you know what she thinks."

Richard III kissed her and said, "Carry to her my true love's kiss; and so, farewell."

Queen Elizabeth exited.

King Richard III, who thought that he had persuaded Queen Elizabeth to persuade her daughter, young Elizabeth of York, to marry him, said about her, "Relenting, soft-hearted fool, and shallow, naïve, changing woman!"

Ratcliff, with Catesby following him, came over to Richard III, who said, "How are you, Ratcliff? What is the news?"

"My gracious sovereign, on the western coast of England rides a powerful navy; to the shore throng many doubt-filled hollow-hearted friends, who are unarmed and who are not determined to beat your enemies back. It is thought that the Earl of Richmond is the navy's admiral, and there they drift, expecting that the forces of Buckingham will welcome them ashore."

"Some swift-footed friend needs to ride to my ally, the Duke of Norfolk," Richard III said. "You yourself, Ratcliff, or Catesby. Where is Catesby?"

"Here I am, my lord."

"Fly to the Duke of Norfolk."

Richard III then said to Ratcliff, "You ride to Salisbury. When you arrive there —"

Seeing Catesby, Richard III said, "Dull, unmindful villain, why are you standing still? Why aren't you on the way to see the Duke of Norfolk?"

"First, mighty sovereign, let me know your mind," Catesby said. "Tell me what message from your grace I shall deliver to him."

"True, good Catesby," Richard III said, "tell him immediately to raise the greatest, strongest, and most powerful army he can, and then to meet me soon at Salisbury."

"I am going now," Catesby said as he exited.

Ratcliff asked Richard III, "What is your highness' pleasure I shall do at Salisbury?"

"Why, what would you do there before I go there?" Richard III asked.

"Your highness told me I should ride there before you do."

"I have changed my mind, sir," Richard III said. "I have changed my mind."

Lord Stanley, the Earl of Derby, arrived and walked over to Richard III.

"How are you?" Richard III asked. "What news have you brought?"

"None so good, my lord, as to please you with the hearing, nor none so bad, but it may well be told."

"A riddle!" Richard III said sarcastically. "Neither good nor bad! Why are you running your mouth so many miles in a circle, when you could tell your tale simply and directly? Once more, what news have you brought?"

"Richmond's navy is on the seas."

"There let him sink, and let the seas be on him!" Richard III said. "That white-livered renegade, what is he doing there?"

"I don't know, mighty sovereign, but I can make a guess," Lord Stanley said.

"Well, sir, since you can make a guess, what guess do you make?"

"Stirred up by Dorset, Buckingham, and the Bishop of Ely, he is making for England, and he intends there to claim the crown."

"Is the throne empty? Is the sword of state unwielded? Is the King dead? Is the empire unpossessed?" Richard III said.

Using the royal plural, he said, "What heir of York is there alive but we? And who is England's King but great York's heir?"

He ignored any claims the House of Lancaster could make to the throne. As far as the House of York — that is, Richard — was concerned, the heir of the third Duke of York, father of Edward IV and of Richard, was still alive. That heir was Richard.

Or he could have meant that he was the heir of the crown from Edward V, who although he was a child who had reigned only from 9 April to 25 June 1483 had been great because he was a King.

Richard III next asked, "So tell me what he is doing upon the sea?"

"Unless for the reason I have already stated, my liege, I cannot guess."

"Unless for the reason that he comes to be your liege, you cannot guess why the Welshman comes," Richard III said.

The Earl of Richmond was Welsh; he was descended from the Welshman Owen Tudor and Katherine of Valois, the widow of King Henry V.

Richard III then said to Lord Stanley, "You will revolt and fly to him, I fear."

"No, I won't, mighty liege," Lord Stanley replied. "Therefore, do not mistrust me."

"Where is your army, then, to beat him back?" Richard III asked. "Where are your tenants and your followers? They should be soldiers opposing the Earl of Richmond. Aren't they now upon the western shore, safely conducting the rebels from their ships?"

"No, my good lord," Lord Stanley said. "My friends are in the north."

"They are cold friends to Richard. What are they doing in the north, when they should be serving their sovereign in the west?"

"They have not been commanded, mighty sovereign, to come and serve you. If it pleases your majesty to give me leave, I'll muster my friends and meet your grace where and at what time your majesty shall please."

"Yes, yes," Richard III replied. "You want to leave so you can join forces with the Earl of Richmond. I will not trust you, sir."

"Most mighty sovereign, you have no cause to doubt my friendship. I never have been and never will be false to you."

"Well, go muster men, but — listen to me carefully — leave behind your son and heir, George Stanley," Richard III said. "Look that your faith to me is firm, or else his head's assurance is frail. If you are not loyal to me, your son will lose his head."

"Deal with him in the same way as I prove true and faithful to you," Lord Stanley said, and then he exited.

A messenger arrived and said, "My gracious sovereign, I am well informed by friends that now in Devonshire several people are in arms against you: Sir Edward Courtney, and the haughty prelate the Bishop of Exeter, his brother there, and many more confederates."

Another messenger arrived and said, "My liege, in Kent the Guildfords are in arms against you, and every hour more confederates flock to their aid, and continually their power increases."

A third messenger arrived and said, "My lord, the army of the Duke of Buckingham —"

Angry, King Richard III said, "Damn you, owls! Do you sing nothing except songs of death?"

The cry of the screech owl was thought to be ominous — an omen of death.

Richard III struck the third messenger and said, "Take that, until you bring me better news."

The third messenger replied, "The news I have to tell your majesty is that because of sudden floods and rainstorms, Buckingham's army has been dispersed and scattered, and Buckingham himself has wandered away alone, no man knows where."

This was good news for Richard III, and he said, "I beg your pardon. Here is some money to cure any injury caused by that blow I gave you. Has any well-advised, prudent friend proclaimed a reward to the man who brings the traitor Buckingham in?"

The third messenger replied, "Such proclamation of a reward has been made, my liege."

A fourth messenger arrived and reported, "It is said, my liege, that Sir Thomas Lovel and Lord Marquess Dorset in Yorkshire are in arms against you. Yet I bring to your grace some good news and comfort. The French navy of the Earl of Richmond has been dispersed by a tempest. Richmond, in Yorkshire, sent out a boat to the shore to ask those on the banks if they were on his side, yes or no. They answered him that they came from Buckingham and were of his party. Richmond, mistrusting them, hoisted sail and set off to return to Brittany, France."

"March on, march on, since we are up in arms," Richard III said. "If don't fight against foreign enemies, yet we can beat down these rebels here at home."

Catesby returned and said, "My liege, the Duke of Buckingham has been captured — that is the best news. That the Earl of Richmond has with a mighty army landed at Milford Haven, on the coast of Wales, is colder tidings, yet they must be told."

"Let's march towards Salisbury!" Richard III said. "While we talk here, a battle to determine who sits on the throne might be won and lost. Someone deliver an order that Buckingham be brought to Salisbury; the rest march on with me."

In the house of Lord Stanley, the Earl of Derby, Sir Christopher Urswick and Lord Stanley talked.

Lord Stanley said, "Sir Christopher, tell the Earl of Richmond this from me. In the sty of this most bloody boar named Richard, my son and heir, George Stanley, is imprisoned and under guard. If I revolt against Richard, off goes young George's head. The fear of that keeps me from offering aid to Richmond right now."

The Earl of Richmond was Lord Stanley's stepson.

Lord Stanley added, "But, tell me, where is Princely Richmond now?"

"He is at Pembroke, or at Haverfordwest, in Wales."

"What men of name — men with titles — resort to him?"

"Sir Walter Herbert, who is a renowned soldier, as well as Sir Gilbert Talbot, Sir William Stanley, the Earl of Oxford, respected Pembroke, Sir James Blunt, and Rice ap Thomas with a valiant crew. Also, many more of noble fame and worth."

"Ap" was part of some Welsh surnames.

Sir Christopher added, "They will march toward London if they don't encounter any resistance. If they do encounter resistance, they will fight."

Lord Stanley said, "Return to Richmond, your lord. Give him my greetings. Tell him that Queen Elizabeth has heartily consented that he shall marry her daughter, young Elizabeth of York."

He handed Sir Christopher Urswick a letter and said, "This letter will inform him about what I think. Farewell."

CHAPTER 5

— 5.1 —

In a field of Salisbury, the Sheriff and some halberdiers led Buckingham to the place of execution.

"Won't King Richard let me speak with him?" Buckingham asked.

"No, my good lord," the Sheriff replied. "Therefore be patient."

"Hastings, and Edward IV's children, Rivers, Grey, Holy King Henry VI, and King Henry VI's fair son — Edward, Prince of Wales — as well as Vaughan, and all others who have died because of underhand, corrupted, foul injustice, if your angry, discontented souls do through the clouds behold this present hour, get your revenge by mocking my destruction!" Buckingham said.

He then asked, "This is All-Souls' Day, fellows, is it not?"

"It is, my lord," the Sheriff said.

On All-Souls' Day, Catholics pray for the souls of the dead, including souls in Purgatory.

"Why, then All-Souls' Day is my body's doomsday — it is my final day," Buckingham said. "This is the doomsday that, in King Edward IV's time, I wished that might fall on me, if I was ever found to be false and disloyal to his children or to his wife's allies. This is the day on which I wished to fall by the false faith of the man I most trusted — Richard.

"This All-Souls' Day to my frightened soul is the appointed day on which the respite for the punishment of my sins ends. That high All-Seer Whom I trifled with has turned my feigned prayer on my head and given to me in earnest what I begged for in jest.

"Thus does He — God — force the swords of wicked men to turn their own points on the wicked men's bosoms. Now old Queen Margaret's curse has fallen upon my head. 'When Richard,' said she, 'shall split your heart with sorrow, remember that Margaret was a prophetess.'

"Come, sirs, convey me to the block of shame where my head will be cut off. Wrong has only wrong, and blame is the due of blame. I have done wrong, and so I will suffer wrong. I am blameworthy, and so I will be blamed."

— 5.2 —

At their camp near Tamworth in central England, the Earl of Richmond stood with some of his followers: the Earl of Oxford, Sir James Blunt, Sir Walter Herbert, and others. Near them were drummers and flag-bearers.

Using the royal plural, the Earl of Richmond said, "Fellows in arms, and my most loving friends, bruised underneath the yoke of tyranny, thus far into the middle of the land have we marched on without impediment and resistance and here we receive from our stepfather, Lord Stanley, some lines of fair comfort and encouragement in a letter.

"The wretched, bloody, and usurping boar — Richard — spoiled your summer fields and fruitful vines. He also swills your warm blood like hogwash and makes his trough in your disemboweled bodies. This foul swine lies now even in the center of this isle, near the town of Leicester, as we learn. From Tamworth to Leicester is only one day's march.

"In God's name, let us cheerfully go on, courageous friends, so we can reap the harvest of perpetual peace by this one bloody trial of sharp war."

Oxford replied, "Every man's conscience is a thousand swords that will fight against that bloody homicide — Richard."

Herbert said, "I don't doubt that Richard's friends will fly to join us."

Blunt said, "Richard has no friends but those who are loyal to him out of fear of what he will do to them if they are not loyal. When he needs their help most, they will shrink from him."

The Earl of Richmond replied, "All of this is to our advantage. So then, in God's name, march. True hope is swift, and flies with swallow's wings. Kings it makes gods, and creatures of lower status it makes Kings."

On a field in Bosworth, where the battle would be fought the following day, stood the fully armed King Richard III. With him were the Duke of Norfolk, the Earl of Suffolk, and others.

King Richard III ordered, "Here pitch our tents, here in Bosworth field."

He then asked, "My Lord of Surrey, why do you look so sad?"

"My heart is ten times lighter than my looks," the Earl of Surrey replied.

"My Lord of Norfolk —" Richard III said.

"I am here, most gracious liege."

"Norfolk, we must have blows in battle, ha! Mustn't we?"

"We must both give and take blows, my gracious lord," the Duke of Norfolk replied.

"Put my tent up there!" Richard III ordered. "I lie here tonight, but where will I lie tomorrow? Well, all's one for that. It doesn't matter."

He then asked, "Who has reconnoitered the number of the foe?"

"Six or seven thousand is their utmost power," the Duke of Norfolk replied.

"Why, the number of soldiers in our battalion triples that number," Richard III said. "Besides, the King's name is a tower of strength, which they in the adverse party lack."

He ordered for the third time, "Up with my tent there!"

Then he said, "Valiant gentlemen, let us survey the battlefield to see which part is most advantageous to place our troops. Call for some men of sound tactical knowledge. Let's lack no discipline and make no delay, for, lords, tomorrow is a busy day."

On the other side of the battlefield, Richmond stood with Sir William Brandon, the Earl of Oxford, and others. Some soldiers were pitching his tent.

Richmond said, "The weary Sun has made a golden set, and by the bright track of his fiery chariot, gives token of a good day tomorrow.

"Sir William Brandon, you shall bear my standard — my flag.

"Give me some ink and paper in my tent. I'll draw the form and layout of our army, appoint each leader to his individual charge, and share in just proportion our small strength.

"My Lord of Oxford, and you, Sir William Brandon, and you, Sir Walter Herbert, stay with me.

"The Earl of Pembroke is staying with his regiment. Good Captain Blunt, bear my 'good night' to him and tell him that by the second hour in the morning I want him to go to my tent and see me. Yet one thing more, good Blunt, before you go, where is Lord Stanley quartered — do you know?"

"Unless I have greatly mistaken his colors — battle flags — which I am very sure I have not done, his regiment lies half a mile at least south from the mighty army of King Richard III."

"If it is possible to do without great danger, good Captain Blunt, bear my 'good night' to him, and give him from me this very important letter."

"Upon my life, my lord, I'll undertake the task," Sir James Blunt replied, "and so, God give you quiet rest tonight!"

"Good night, good Captain Blunt," Richmond said. "Come, gentlemen, let us plan tomorrow's business inside our tent; the air is raw and cold."

On the other side of the battlefield, the Duke of Norfolk, Ratcliff, Catesby, and others went to Richard III, who asked, "What time is it?"

"It's suppertime, my lord," Catesby replied. "It's nine o'clock."

It was late for suppertime, but Catesby knew that Richard III had not eaten.

"I will not have supper tonight," Richard III said. "Give me some ink and paper. Is the beaver of my helmet easier to manipulate than it was? And is all my armor laid in my tent?"

"It is, my liege," Catesby replied. "All things are in readiness."

"Good Norfolk, hasten to your charge," Richard III said. "Put up careful watch, choose trusty sentinels."

"I go, my lord," the Duke of Norfolk replied.

"Get up with the morning lark tomorrow, noble Norfolk," Richard III said.

"I promise you that I will, my lord."

He exited.

"Catesby!" Richard III called.

"My lord?" Catesby replied.

"Send out a Pursuivant-at-Arms to Lord Stanley's regiment. Tell him to bring his army before the Sun rises, lest George, his son, fall into the blind cave of eternal night. If Lord Stanley fails to obey my order, his son will die."

A Pursuivant-at-Arms is a junior officer who attends a herald.

Catesby exited.

Richard III ordered, "Fill me a bowl of wine. Give me a clock. Saddle my horse, which is named White Surrey, for the battlefield tomorrow. Look that my lances are sound, and not too heavy."

He then called, "Ratcliff!"

"My lord?" Ratcliff replied.

"Have you seen the melancholy Lord Northumberland?" Richard III asked.

"The Earl of Surrey and he, at around twilight, the time for shutting away chickens, went from troop to troop through the army, cheering up the soldiers."

"I am satisfied," Richard III said. "Give me a bowl of wine: I don't have that brisk readiness of spirit, nor cheerfulness of mind, that I used to have. Set the wine down. Are ink and paper ready?"

"They are, my lord," Ratcliff replied.

"Tell my guard to keep watch; leave me. Ratcliff, about the middle of the night come to my tent and help to arm me. Leave me, I say."

Ratcliff and Richard III's attendants departed, leaving the guard behind.

On the other side of the battlefield, Lord Stanley, the Earl of Derby, went to visit the Earl of Richmond. This was a secret meeting between stepfather and stepson because Lord Stanley was supposed to fight for Richard III during the upcoming battle.

Lord Stanley said, "May fortune and victory guide your destiny! May you be victorious tomorrow!"

"May all the comfort that the dark night can afford be yours, noble stepfather!" Richmond replied.

Using the royal plural, he said, "Tell me, how is our loving mother?"

"I, as your mother's deputy, bless you from your mother, who prays continually for your good. So much for that. The silent hours steal on, and flakes of darkness break in the East.

"In brief — for the time bids us to be brief — prepare your army early in the morning, and put your fortune to the arbitration of bloody sword strokes and death-dealing war.

"I, as I may — that which I would like to do, which is to support you openly, I cannot — will as best I can secretly support your side and aid you in this doubtful and feasome shock of arms. But I may not be too openly on your side lest, if I am seen supporting you, your stepbrother, young George, be executed in his father's sight.

"Farewell. The lack of leisure time and the fears of this time cut off the ceremonious vows of love and ample interchange of sweet discourse, which family members as long separated as we should dwell upon. May God give us leisure for these rites of love! Once more, adieu. Be valiant, and prosper well!"

Richmond ordered, "Good lords, conduct Lord Stanley to his regiment. I'll strive, with troubled thoughts, to take a nap, lest leaden slumber weigh me down tomorrow, when I should mount with wings of victory. Once more, good night, kind lords and gentlemen."

Everyone except Richmond exited.

He prayed, "Oh, You, Whose captain I account myself, look on my military forces with a gracious eye; put in their hands Your bruising irons of wrath, so that they may crush with a heavy fall the usurping helmets of our adversaries! Make us Your ministers of chastisement, so that we may praise You in the victory! To You I commend my watchful soul, before I let fall the windows — the eyelids — of my eyes. Sleeping and waking, defend me always!"

He fell asleep.

On the opposite side of the battlefield, Richard III was also asleep.

Ghosts began to appear in the dreams of King Richard III and the Earl of Richmond.

The ghost of Prince Edward, son of King Henry VI, appeared.

To Richard III, he said, "Let me sit heavy on your soul tomorrow! Think about how you stabbed me in the prime of my youth at Tewksbury. Despair, therefore, and die!"

To Richmond, he said, "Be cheerful, Richmond; for the wronged souls of butchered Princes fight in your behalf. King Henry VI's son thus comforts you, Richmond."

The ghost of King Henry VI appeared.

To Richard III, he said, "When I was mortal, my anointed body was punched full of deadly holes by you. Think about the Tower of London and me. Despair, and die! Harry VI tells you to despair, and die!"

To Richmond, he said, "Virtuous and holy, you will be conqueror! Harry, who prophesied that you would be King, thus comforts you in your sleep. Live, and flourish!"

The ghost of Clarence appeared.

To Richard III, he said, "Let me sit heavy on your soul tomorrow! I, who was washed to death with nauseating wine, am poor Clarence, who by your guile was betrayed to death! Tomorrow in the battle think about me, and drop your blunt sword. Despair, and die!"

To Richmond, he said, "You offspring of the House of Lancaster, the wronged heirs of the House of York pray for you. May good angels guard your army! Live, and flourish!"

The ghosts of Rivers, Grey, and Vaughan appeared.

Rivers said, "Let me sit heavy on your soul tomorrow. I am Rivers, who died at Pomfret! Despair, and die!"

Grey said to Richard III, "Think about Grey, and let your soul despair!"

Vaughan said to Richard III, "Think about Vaughan, and with guilty fear, let your lance drop. Despair, and die!"

All together, the three ghosts said to Richmond, "Awaken, and think that our wrongs in Richard's bosom will conquer him! Awaken, and win the day!"

The ghost of Hastings appeared.

Hastings said to Richard III, "Bloodthirsty and guilty, guiltily awaken, and in a bloody battle end your days! Think about Lord Hastings. Despair, and die!"

To Richmond he said, "Quiet untroubled soul, awaken, awaken! Arm, fight, and conquer, for fair England's sake!"

The ghosts of the two young Princes appeared.

To Richard III they said together, "Dream about your nephews who were smothered in the Tower of London. Let us be led within your bosom, Richard, and weigh you down to ruin, shame, and death! Your nephews' souls tell you to despair and die!"

To Richmond they said, "Sleep, Richmond, sleep in peace, and wake in joy. May good angels guard you from the boar's annoyance! Live, and beget a happy race of Kings! Edward IV's unhappy sons tell you to flourish."

The ghost of Lady Anne appeared.

To Richard III she said, "Richard, your wife, that wretched Anne who never slept a quiet hour with you, now fills your sleep with perturbations. Tomorrow in the battle think about me, and drop your blunt sword. Despair, and die!"

To Richmond she said, "You quiet soul, sleep a quiet sleep. Dream of success and happy victory! Your adversary's wife prays for you."

The ghost of Buckingham appeared.

To Richard III he said, "I was the first who helped you to the crown; I was the last who felt your tyranny. In the battle think about Buckingham, and die in terror of your guiltiness! Dream on, dream on, dream of bloody deeds and death. Fainting, despair; despairing, yield your breath!"

To Richmond he said, "I died because I hoped to render you aid before I was able to yield you aid. But cheer your heart, and do not be dismayed. May God and good angels fight on Richmond's side, and may Richard fall from the height of all his pride."

The ghosts vanished.

Still half-asleep, Richard III called, "Give me another horse! Bind up my wounds! Have mercy, Jesus!"

He woke up and said, "Wait! I was only dreaming. Coward conscience, how you are afflicting me! The candle flames burn blue — a sign of the presence of ghosts. It is now exactly midnight. Cold fearful drops — tears — stand on my trembling flesh.

"What do I fear? Myself? There's no one else nearby. Richard loves Richard; that is, I am I. Is there a murderer here? No. Yes, a murderer is here because I am here. Then fly away from here. What, from myself? Here is a great reason why I should flee from myself — lest I get revenge on myself. What, revenge myself upon myself? Alas. I love myself. Why? For any good that I myself have done to myself? No! Instead, I hate myself because of the hateful deeds committed by myself! I am a villain. Yet I lie. I am not a villain. Fool, of yourself speak well. Fool, do not flatter yourself.

"My conscience has a thousand different tongues, and every tongue brings in a different tale, and every tale condemns me for a villain. Perjury, perjury, in the highest degree. Murder, stern murder, in the direst degree. All different kinds of sins, all used in each degree — bad, worse, worst — throng to the bar of justice, all of them crying, 'Guilty! Guilty!'

"I shall despair. No creature loves me, and if I die, no soul shall pity me. Why should they, since I myself find in myself no pity for myself? I thought that the souls of all whom I had murdered came to my tent, and every soul threatened vengeance tomorrow on the head of me, Richard."

Ratcliff arrived and said, "My lord!"

"By God's wounds! Who is there?" Richard III said.

"Ratcliff, my lord; it is I. The early village rooster has twice crowed and saluted the morning. Your friends are up and buckle on their armor."

"Ratcliff, I have dreamed a frightening dream!" Richard III said. "What do you think? Will all our friends prove to be true and loyal?"

"No doubt, my lord."

"Ratcliff, I fear, I fear —"

"No, my good lord, do not be afraid of shadows."

Richard III replied, "By the apostle Paul, shadows tonight have struck more terror to the soul of Richard than can the substance of ten thousand soldiers armed in proven-to-be-impenetrable armor, and led by shallow Richmond. It is not yet near day. Come, go with me. Under our tents I'll play the eavesdropper in order to see if any soldiers mean to desert me."

On the other side of the battlefield, some lords went to Richmond's tent.

"Good morning, Richmond!" they said.

"I beg your pardon, lords and wakeful gentlemen," Richmond said. "You have found me acting like a tardy sluggard here."

A lord asked, "How have you slept, my lord?"

"Since your departure, my lords, I have enjoyed the sweetest sleep, and the fairest-boding, most encouraging dreams that ever entered a drowsy head. I dreamed that the souls whose bodies Richard murdered came to my tent, and shouted 'Victory' to me. I promise you that my soul is very joyful as it remembers so fair a dream."

He then asked, "How late in the morning is it, lords?"

"It is almost the stroke of four."

"Why, then it is time for me to arm and give orders," Richmond said.

He said to his soldiers, "Loving countrymen, the lack of time available before we fight forbids me to say much more than I have already said, but remember this. God and our good cause fight upon our side. The prayers of holy saints and wronged souls, like high-reared fortified walls, stand before our faces. With the exception of Richard, those whom we fight against prefer to have us win than Richard, whom they follow.

"For what is the man whom they follow? Truly, gentlemen, he is a bloodthirsty tyrant and a murderer. He is a man who was raised to the throne because of bloodshed, and a man who has kept the throne because of bloodshed. He is a man who used people to get what he has, and he slaughtered those who were the means to help him achieve the throne.

"He is a base and foul stone, made precious only by the foil of England's throne, where he is falsely set."

Richmond was comparing Richard to a stone of little worth — Richard was not a precious jewel — that had been placed in a foil, or setting, of great worth.

Richmond continued, "Richard is a man who has always been God's enemy. If you fight against God's enemy, God will justly protect you as his soldiers. If you sweat to put a tyrant down, you will sleep in peace once the tyrant is slain. If you fight against your country's foes, your country's fat — its wealth — shall pay the wage for your pains. If you fight to keep your wives safe, your wives shall welcome home the conquerors. If you free your children from the sword, your children's children will repay you in your old age.

"So then, in the name of God and all these rights, raise high your flags, draw your willing swords. As for me, the ransom of my bold attempt to save England from Richard shall be this cold corpse on the Earth's cold face. If I am captured, I shall pay no ransom to be freed — Richard will have to kill me. But if I thrive, the least of you shall share in the gain of my attempt to save England from Richard.

"Play the drums and trumpets boldly and cheerfully. God and Saint George! Richmond and victory!"

On the other side of the battlefield, King Richard III and Ratcliff spoke. With them were attendants and soldiers.

"What did Northumberland say about Richmond?" Richard III asked.

"That he was never trained as a soldier," Ratcliff answered.

"He said the truth, and what did Surrey say then?"

"He smiled and said, 'The better for our purpose.'"

"He was in the right; and so indeed it is," Richard III said.

A clock began to strike, and Richard III said, "Count the strokes."

After the clock had finished striking, he said, "Give me an almanac. Who has seen the Sun today?"

"Not I, my lord," Ratcliff replied.

After looking at the almanac, Richard III said, "Then he — the Sun — disdains to shine; for according to the almanac, he should have adorned the East an hour ago. A black day will it be to somebody. Ratcliff!"

"My lord?"

"The Sun will not be seen today," Richard III said. "The sky frowns and scowls upon our army. I wish these dewy tears were off the ground — I wish the Sun would dry the dew. Not shine today! Why, what is that to me more than it is to Richmond? The same Heaven that frowns on me looks sadly upon him."

The Duke of Norfolk arrived and said, "Arm, arm, my lord; the foe vaunts and exults in the field."

"Come, bustle, bustle," Richard III said. "Caparison and make ready my horse; put my horse's trappings on it. Call up Lord Stanley and tell him to bring his army."

He then pointed to a map as he said, "I will lead forth my soldiers to the plain, and my army shall be ordered like this. My front line of soldiers shall be drawn out all in length, consisting equally of cavalry and infantry. Our archers shall be placed in their midst. John, Duke of Norfolk, and Thomas, Earl of Surrey, shall lead these foot soldiers and horse soldiers. They thus deployed, I will follow with our main forces, which on either side shall be well flanked with our best cavalry. We will have all this and the help of Saint George to boot! What do you think, Norfolk?"

"This is a good plan, warlike sovereign," the Duke of Norfolk replied. He then showed Richard III a piece of paper and said, "I found this on my tent this morning."

Richard III read the piece of paper out loud, "Jockey of Norfolk, be not too bold, for Dickon your master is bought and sold."

"Jockey" was a nickname for John; John was the Christian name of the Duke of Norfolk. "Dickon" was a nickname for Richard. "To be bought and sold" meant "to be betrayed for money or something of worth."

Richard III said, "This is a thing devised by the enemy. Go, gentleman, every man go to his charge. Let not our babbling dreams frighten our souls. Conscience is only a word that cowards use; it was first invented to keep the strong in awe. Let our strong arms be our conscience, and let our swords be our law. March on, join bravely, let us go pell-mell if not to Heaven, then hand in hand to Hell."

"What shall I say more than I have said? Remember with whom you are to cope. They are a sort of vagabonds, rascals, and runaways. They are a scum of Bretons from Brittany, France, and they are base lackey peasants, whom their over-filled country vomits forth and so they go to desperate ventures and assured destruction.

"You sleeping safe, they bring to you unrest. You having lands, and blest with beauteous wives, they would steal the one, and stain the other.

"And who leads them but a paltry fellow, long kept in Brittany at our brother-in-law's cost?"

Charles, Duke of Burgundy, had financially supported the Earl of Richmond at the court of the Duke of Brittany. King Richard III's sister, Margaret of York, had married Charles, Duke of Burgundy.

Richard III continued, "He is a milk-sop, one who never in his life felt as much cold as is felt by one standing in snow higher than his shoes. Let's whip these stragglers over the seas again; let's lash away from here these overweening rags of France, these famished beggars, who are weary of their lives, and who, poor rats, except for dreaming on this foolish exploit, would hang themselves because they lack the means of supporting their lives."

He was comparing Richmond's soldiers to poor vagabonds who, if they were found wandering outside their own parish, would be whipped and sent back to their parish.

Richard III continued, "If we shall be conquered, let men conquer us, and not these bastard Bretons, whom our fathers have in their own land beaten, struck, and thumped, and left them the heirs of shame in the history books."

He was referring to English victories over the French. In 1346, on a French battlefield, Edward the Black Prince, the son of King Edward III, played the role of a hero as he and his soldiers defeated the French army in the Battle of Crécy. In 1356, he also defeated the French in the Battle of Poitiers. On 25 October 1415, on the plains near the village of Agincourt, King Henry V and his army, despite being vastly outnumbered, decisively defeated the French army.

Richard III continued, "Shall these Bretons enjoy our lands? Shall they lie with our wives? Shall they rape our daughters?"

Military drums sounded.

Richard III continued, "Listen! I hear their drums. Fight, gentlemen of England! Fight, bold yoemen! Draw, archers, draw your arrows until the arrowhead touches the bent bow! Spur your proud horses hard, and ride in full vigor and in blood from your spurs. Amaze the sky with your lances that break as they hit their target!"

A messenger entered, and King Richard III asked, "What does Lord Stanley say? Will he bring his army?"

"My lord, he says that he will not come."

"Off with the head of George, his son and heir!" Richard III shouted.

The Duke of Norfolk said, "My lord, the enemy has advanced past the marsh. Let George Stanley die after the battle."

Richard III said, "A thousand hearts are great within my bosom. Raise our flags, set upon our foes. May our ancient word of courage, fair Saint George, inspire us with the spleen of fiery dragons! Let us set upon them! Victory steers our course."

In the middle of the battle, Catesby shouted for help for King Richard III, "Rescue, my Lord of Norfolk, rescue, rescue! The King performs more wonders than seems possible for a man! He dares every opponent to fight to the death! His horse has been slain, and he is fighting on foot, seeking Richmond in the throat of death! Rescue, fair lord, or else the day is lost!"

King Richard III appeared and shouted, "A horse! A horse! My Kingdom for a horse!"

He did not want to flee; he knew that he could fight more valiantly on horseback.

Catesby said, "Withdraw, my lord; I'll help you to find a horse."

Richard III was unwilling to withdraw from the battle; he wanted to fight.

He replied, "Slave, I have set my life upon a cast of the die, and I will stand the hazard of the die, win or lose. I think six Richmonds are on the battlefield; I have slain five copies today instead of the real Richmond. Those five copies were dressed like Richmond to fool me."

He then shouted, "A horse! A horse! My Kingdom for a horse!"

Later, King Richard III and the real Richmond met on the battlefield, and Richmond killed Richard III. Fighting continued until a retreat was sounded, and Richmond and his army were victorious. Now he stood on the battlefield with many lords, including Lord Stanley, Earl of Derby, who was holding the crown.

Richmond said, "God and your arms be praised, victorious friends. The day is ours; the bloodthirsty dog — Richard — is dead."

Lord Stanley said, "Courageous Richmond, you have acquitted yourself well. Look here, I have plucked off this long-usurped crown from the dead temples of this bloody wretch so that you can grace your brows with it. Wear it, enjoy it, and make much of it."

"Great God of Heaven, say 'Amen' to all!" Richmond said. "But, tell me, is young George Stanley living?"

Lord Stanley, George's father, replied, "He is, my lord, and he is safe in Leicester, where, if it pleases you, we may now go."

"What men of high rank are slain on either side?"

Lord Stanley replied, "John, the Duke of Norfolk; Walter Lord Ferrers, Sir Robert Brakenbury, and Sir William Brandon."

"Inter their bodies as is suitable for their births," Richmond said. Using the royal plural, he said, "Proclaim a pardon to the enemy soldiers who fled and who will in submission return to us. We took the sacrament when we vowed to marry young Elizabeth of York, and together she and I will unite the white and the red."

He meant that by marrying young Elizabeth of York, he and she would unite the House of York and the House of Lancaster. The emblem of the House of York is a white rose, and the emblem of the House of Lancaster is a red rose. The marriage would end the enmity between the two Houses and bring peace to England. He would also be the first Tudor King.

He continued, "May Heaven smile upon this fair conjunction, this marriage; Heaven has long frowned on the enmity between the two Houses! What traitor hears me, and does not say, 'Amen'?

"England has long been mad, and scarred herself. The brother has blindly shed the brother's blood. The father has rashly slaughtered his own son. The son has been forced to butcher the sire. All this divided York and Lancaster; they were divided in their dire division, for the divided Houses led to other divisions.

"Now let Richmond and Elizabeth, the true successors of each royal House, by God's fair ordinance join together! And let their heirs, God, if Your will be so, enrich the time to come with smooth-faced peace, with smiling plenty, and with fair prosperous days!

"Dull the swords of traitors, gracious Lord, who would bring these bloody days again, and make poor England weep in streams of blood! Let those who would with treason wound this fair land's peace not live to taste this land's prosperity!

"Now civil wounds are closed up, and now peace lives again. So that she may long live here, may God say, 'Amen!'"

Appendix A: Brief Historical Background

KING EDWARD I: 1272-1307

Edward Longshanks fought and defeated the Welsh chieftains, and he made his eldest son the Prince of Wales. He won victories against the Scots, and he brought the coronation stone from Scone to Westminster.

KING EDWARD II: 1307-deposed 1327

At the Battle of Bannockburn in 1314, the Scots defeated his army. His wife and her lover, Mortimer, deposed him. According to legend, he was murdered in Berkeley Castle by means of a red-hot poker thrust up his anus.

KING EDWARD III: 1327-1377

Son of King Edward II, he reigned for a long time — 50 years. Because he wanted to conquer Scotland and France, he started the Hundred Years War in 1338. King Edward III and his eldest son, Edward the Black Prince, won important victories against the French in the Battle of Crécy (1346) and the Battle of Poitiers (1356).

One of King Edward III's sons was John of Gaunt, first Duke of Lancaster.

Another of King Edward III's sons was Edmund of Langley, first Duke of York.

During his reign, the Black Death — the bubonic plague — struck in 1348-1350 and killed half of England's population.

KING RICHARD II: 1377-deposed 1399

King Richard II was the son of Edward the Black Prince. In 1381, Wat Tyler led the Peasants Revolt, which was suppressed. King Richard II sent Henry, Duke of Lancaster, into exile and seized Henry's estates, but in 1399 Henry, Duke of Lancaster, returned from exile and deposed King Richard II, thereby becoming King Henry IV. In 1400, King Richard II was murdered in Pontefract Castle, which is also known as Pomfret Castle.

HOUSE OF LANCASTER

KING HENRY IV: 1399-1413

Henry, Duke of Lancaster, was the son of John of Gaunt, who was the third son of King Edward III. He was born at Bolingbroke Castle and so was also known as Henry of Bolingbroke. Returning from exile in France to reclaim his estates, he deposed King Richard II. He spent the 13 years of his reign putting down rebellions and defending himself against those who would assassinate or depose him. The Welshman Owen Glendower and the English Percy family were among those who fought against him. King Henry IV died at the age of 45.

KING HENRY V: 1413-1422

The son of King Henry IV, King Henry V renewed the war with France. He and his army defeated the French at the Battle of Agincourt (1415) despite being heavily outnumbered. He married Catherine of Valoise, the daughter of the French King, but he died before becoming King of France. He left behind a 10-month-old son, who became King Henry VI.

KING HENRY VI: 1422-deposed 1461; briefly returned to the throne in 1470-1471

The Hundred Years War ended in 1453; the English lost all land in France except for Calais, a port city. After King Henry VI suffered an attack of mental illness in 1454, Richard, third Duke of York and the father of King Henry IV and King Richard III, was made Protector of the Realm. England suffered civil war after the House of York challenged King Henry VI's right to be King of England. In 1470, King Henry VI was briefly restored to the English throne. In 1471, he was murdered in the Tower of London. A short time previously, his son, Edward, Prince of Wales, had been killed at the Battle of Tewkesbury in 1471; this was the final battle in the Wars of the Roses. The Yorkists decisively defeated the Lancastrians.

King Henry VI founded both Eton College and King's College, Cambridge.

WARS OF THE ROSES

From 1455-1487, the Yorkists and the Lancastrians fought for power in England in the famous Wars of the Roses. The emblem of the York family was a white rose, and the emblem of the Lancaster family was a red rose. The Yorkists and the Lancastrians were descended from King Edward III.

HOUSE OF YORK

KING EDWARD IV: 1461-1483 (King Henry VI briefly returned to the throne in 1470-1471)

Son of Richard, third Duke of York, he charged his brother George, Duke of Clarence, with treason and had him murdered in 1478. After dying suddenly, he left behind two sons aged 12 and 9, and five daughters.

His surviving two brothers in Shakespeare's play *Richard III* are these: 1) George, Duke of Clarence. Clarence is the second-oldest brother; and 2) Richard, Duke of Gloucester, and afterwards King Richard III. Gloucester is the youngest surviving brother.

William Caxton established the first printing press in Westminster during King Edward IV's reign.

KING EDWARD V: 1483-1483

The eldest son of King Edward IV, he reigned for only two months, the shortest-lived monarch in English history. He was 13 years old. He and his younger brother, Richard, were murdered in the Tower of London. According to Shakespeare's play, their uncle, Richard, Duke of Gloucester, who became King Richard III, was responsible for their murders.

KING RICHARD III: 1483-1485

Brother of King Edward IV, Richard, the Duke of Gloucester, declared the two Princes in the Tower of London — King Edward V and Richard, Duke of York — illegitimate and made himself King Richard III. In 1485, Henry Tudor, Earl of Richmond, a descendant of John of Gaunt, who was the father of King Henry IV, defeated King Richard III at the Battle of Bosworth Field in Leicestershire. King Richard III died in that battle.

King Richard III's father was Richard Plantagenet, Duke of York. His mother was Cecily Neville, Duchess of York.

King Richard III's death in the Battle of Bosworth Field is regarded as marking the end of the Middle Ages in England.

A NOTE ON THE PLANTAGENETS

The first Plantagenet King was King Henry II (1154-1189). From 1154 until 1485, when King Richard III died, all English kings were Plantagenets. Both the Lancaster family and the York family were Plantagenets.

Geoffrey Plantagenet, Count of Anjou, was the founder of the House of Plantagenet. Geoffrey's son, Henry Curtmantle, became King Henry II of England, thereby founding the Plantagenet dynasty. Geoffrey wore a sprig of broom, a flowering shrub, as a badge; the Latin name for broom is *planta genista*, and from it the name "Plantagenet" arose.

The Plantagenet dynasty can be divided into three parts:

1154-1216: The Angevins. The Angevin Kings were Henry II, Richard I (Richard the Lionheart), and John 1.

1216-1399: The Plantagenets. These Kings ranged from King Henry III to King Richard II.

1399-1485: The Houses of Lancaster and of York. These Kings ranged from King Henry IV to King Richard III.

BEGINNING OF THE TUDOR DYNASTY

KING HENRY VII: 1485-1509

When King Richard III fell at the Battle of Bosworth, Henry Tudor, Earl of Richmond, became King Henry VII. A Lancastrian, he married Elizabeth of York — young Elizabeth of York in *Richard III* — and united the two warring houses, York and Lancaster, thus ending the Wars of the Roses. One of his grandfathers was Sir Owen Tudor, who married Catherine of Valoise, widow of King Henry V.

KING HENRY VIII: 1509-1547

King Henry VIII had six wives. These are their fates: "Divorced, Beheaded, Died, Divorced, Beheaded, Survived." He divorced his first wife, Catherine of Aragon, so that he could marry Anne Boleyn. Because of this, England divorced itself from the Catholic Church, and King Henry VIII became the head of the Church of England. King Henry VIII had one son and two daughters, all of whom became rulers of England: Edward, daughter of Jane Seymour; Mary, daughter of Catherine of Aragon; and Elizabeth, daughter of Anne Boleyn.

KING EDWARD VI: 1547-1553

The son of Henry VIII and Jane Seymour, King Edward VI succeeded his father at the age of nine; a Council of Regency with his uncle, Duke of Somerset, styled Protector, ruled the government.

During King Edward VI's reign, Archbishop Thomas Cranmer wrote the 1549 Book of Common Prayer.

When King Edward VI died, Lady Jane Grey was proclaimed Queen, but she ruled for only nine days before being executed in 1554, aged 17. Mary, daughter of Catherine of Aragon, became Queen. She was Catholic, thus the attempt to make Lady Jane Grey, a Protestant, Queen.

QUEEN MARY I (BLOODY MARY) 1553-1558

Queen Mary I attempted to make England a Catholic nation again. Some Protestant bishops, including Archbishop Thomas Cranmer, were burnt at the stake, and other violence broke out, resulting in her being known as Bloody Mary.

QUEEN ELIZABETH I: 1558-1603

The daughter of King Henry VIII and Anne Boleyn, Queen Elizabeth I was a popular Queen. In 1588, the English navy decisively defeated the Spanish Armada. England had many notable playwrights and poets, including William Shakespeare and Ben Jonson, during her reign. She never married and had no children.

KING JAMES I OF ENGLAND: A MEMBER OF THE HOUSE OF STUART

KING JAMES I OF ENGLAND AND VI OF SCOTLAND: 1603-1625

King James I of England was the son of Mary, Queen of Scots, and Lord Darnley. In 1605 Guy Fawkes and his Catholic co-conspirators were captured before they could blow up the Houses of Parliament; this was known as the Gunpowder Plot.

In 1611, during King James I's reign, the Authorized Version of the Bible (the King James Version) was completed.

Also during King James I's reign, in 1620 the Pilgrims sailed for America in their ship *The Mayflower*.

A NOTE ON SHAKESPEARE

When William Shakespeare (1564-1616) wrote *Richard III*, Queen Elizabeth I was on the throne. She was a Tudor, a fact that may have influenced Shakespeare to make King Richard III more evil than he perhaps was. Shakespeare lived under two monarchs: Queen Elizabeth I and King James I.

Appendix B: About the Author

It was a dark and stormy night. Suddenly a cry rang out, and on a hot summer night in 1954, Josephine, wife of Carl Bruce, gave birth to a boy — me. Unfortunately, this young married couple allowed Reuben Saturday, Josephine's brother, to name their first-born. Reuben, aka "The Joker," decided that Bruce was a nice name, so he decided to name me Bruce Bruce. I have gone by my middle name — David — ever since.

Being named Bruce David Bruce hasn't been all bad. Bank tellers remember me very quickly, so I don't often have to show an ID. It can be fun in charades, also. When I was a counselor as a teenager at Camp Echoing Hills in Warsaw, Ohio, a fellow counselor gave the signs for "sounds like" and "two words," then she pointed to a bruise on her leg twice. Bruise Bruise? Oh yeah, Bruce Bruce is the answer!

Uncle Reuben, by the way, gave me a haircut when I was in kindergarten. He cut my hair short and shaved a small bald spot on the back of my head. My mother wouldn't let me go to school until the bald spot grew out again.

Of all my brothers and sisters (six in all), I am the only transplant to Athens, Ohio. I was born in Newark, Ohio, and have lived all around Southeastern Ohio. However, I moved to Athens to go to Ohio University and have never left.

At Ohio U, I never could make up my mind whether to major in English or Philosophy, so I got a bachelor's degree with a double major in both areas, then I added a master's degree in English and a master's degree in Philosophy.

Currently, and for a long time to come (I eat fruits and vegetables), I am spending my retirement writing books such as *Nadia Comaneci: Perfect 10*, *The Funniest People in Dance*, *Homer's* Iliad: *A Retelling in Prose*, and *William Shakespeare's* Othello: *A Retelling in Prose*.

By the way, my sister Brenda Kennedy writes romances such as *A New Beginning* and *Shattered Dreams*.

Appendix C: Some Books by David Bruce

Retellings of a Classic Work of Literature

Arden of Faversham: A Retelling

Ben Jonson's The Alchemist: *A Retelling*

Ben Jonson's The Arraignment, or Poetaster: *A Retelling*

Ben Jonson's Bartholomew Fair: *A Retelling*

Ben Jonson's The Case is Altered: *A Retelling*

Ben Jonson's Catiline's Conspiracy: *A Retelling*

Ben Jonson's The Devil is an Ass: *A Retelling*

Ben Jonson's Epicene: *A Retelling*

Ben Jonson's Every Man in His Humor: *A Retelling*

Ben Jonson's Every Man Out of His Humor: *A Retelling*

Ben Jonson's The Fountain of Self-Love, or Cynthia's Revels: *A Retelling*

Ben Jonson's The Magnetic Lady, or Humors Reconciled: *A Retelling*

Ben Jonson's The New Inn, or The Light Heart: *A Retelling*

Ben Jonson's Sejanus' Fall: *A Retelling*

Ben Jonson's The Staple of News: *A Retelling*

Ben Jonson's A Tale of a Tub: *A Retelling*

Ben Jonson's Volpone, or the Fox: *A Retelling*

Christopher Marlowe's Complete Plays: Retellings

Christopher Marlowe's Dido, Queen of Carthage: *A Retelling*

Christopher Marlowe's Doctor Faustus: *Retellings of the 1604 A-Text and of the 1616 B-Text*

Christopher Marlowe's Edward II: *A Retelling*

Christopher Marlowe's The Massacre at Paris: *A Retelling*

Christopher Marlowe's The Rich Jew of Malta: *A Retelling*

Christopher Marlowe's Tamburlaine, Parts 1 and 2: *Retellings*

Dante's Divine Comedy: *A Retelling in Prose*

Dante's Inferno: *A Retelling in Prose*

Dante's Purgatory: *A Retelling in Prose*

Dante's Paradise: *A Retelling in Prose*

The Famous Victories of Henry V: *A Retelling*

From the Iliad *to the* Odyssey: *A Retelling in Prose of Quintus of Smyrna's* Posthomerica

George Chapman, Ben Jonson, and John Marston's Eastward Ho! *A Retelling*

George Peele's The Arraignment of Paris: *A Retelling*

George Peele's The Battle of Alcazar: *A Retelling*

George's Peele's David and Bathsheba, and the Tragedy of Absalom: *A Retelling*

George Peele's Edward I: *A Retelling*

George Peele's The Old Wives' Tale: *A Retelling*

George-a-Greene: *A Retelling*

The History of King Leir: A Retelling

Homer's Iliad: *A Retelling in Prose*

Homer's Odyssey: *A Retelling in Prose*

J.W. Gent.'s The Valiant Scot: *A Retelling*

Jason and the Argonauts: A Retelling in Prose of Apollonius of Rhodes' Argonautica

John Ford: Eight Plays Translated into Modern English

John Ford's The Broken Heart: *A Retelling*

John Ford's The Fancies, Chaste and Noble: *A Retelling*

John Ford's The Lady's Trial: *A Retelling*

John Ford's The Lover's Melancholy: *A Retelling*

John Ford's Love's Sacrifice: *A Retelling*

John Ford's Perkin Warbeck: *A Retelling*

John Ford's The Queen: *A Retelling*

John Ford's 'Tis Pity She's a Whore: *A Retelling*

John Lyly's Campaspe: *A Retelling*

John Lyly's Endymion, The Man in the Moon: *A Retelling*

John Lyly's Galatea: *A Retelling*

John Lyly's Love's Metamorphosis: *A Retelling*

John Lyly's Midas: *A Retelling*

John Lyly's Mother Bombie: *A Retelling*

John Lyly's Sappho and Phao: *A Retelling*

John Lyly's The Woman in the Moon: *A Retelling*

John Webster's The White Devil: *A Retelling*

King Edward III: *A Retelling*

Mankind: *A Medieval Morality Play* (A Retelling)

Margaret Cavendish's The Unnatural Tragedy: *A Retelling*

The Merry Devil of Edmonton: *A Retelling*

The Summoning of Everyman: *A Medieval Morality Play* (A Retelling)

Robert Greene's Friar Bacon and Friar Bungay: *A Retelling*

The Taming of a Shrew: *A Retelling*

Tarlton's Jests: A Retelling

Thomas Middleton's A Chaste Maid in Cheapside: *A Retelling*

Thomas Middleton's Women Beware Women: *A Retelling*

Thomas Middleton and Thomas Dekker's The Roaring Girl: *A Retelling*

Thomas Middleton and William Rowley's The Changeling: *A Retelling*

The Trojan War and Its Aftermath: Four Ancient Epic Poems

Virgil's Aeneid: *A Retelling in Prose*

William Shakespeare's 5 Late Romances: Retellings in Prose

William Shakespeare's 10 Histories: Retellings in Prose

William Shakespeare's 11 Tragedies: Retellings in Prose

William Shakespeare's 12 Comedies: Retellings in Prose

William Shakespeare's 38 Plays: Retellings in Prose

William Shakespeare's 1 Henry IV, aka Henry IV, Part 1: *A Retelling in Prose*

William Shakespeare's 2 Henry IV, aka Henry IV, Part 2: *A Retelling in Prose*

William Shakespeare's 1 Henry VI, aka Henry VI, Part 1: *A Retelling in Prose*

William Shakespeare's 2 Henry VI, aka Henry VI, Part 2: *A Retelling in Prose*

William Shakespeare's 3 Henry VI, aka Henry VI, Part 3: *A Retelling in Prose*

William Shakespeare's All's Well that Ends Well: *A Retelling in Prose*

William Shakespeare's Antony and Cleopatra: *A Retelling in Prose*

William Shakespeare's As You Like It: *A Retelling in Prose*

William Shakespeare's The Comedy of Errors: *A Retelling in Prose*

William Shakespeare's Coriolanus: *A Retelling in Prose*

William Shakespeare's Cymbeline: *A Retelling in Prose*

William Shakespeare's Hamlet: *A Retelling in Prose*

William Shakespeare's Henry V: *A Retelling in Prose*

William Shakespeare's Henry VIII: *A Retelling in Prose*

William Shakespeare's Julius Caesar: *A Retelling in Prose*

William Shakespeare's King John: *A Retelling in Prose*

William Shakespeare's King Lear: *A Retelling in Prose*

William Shakespeare's Love's Labor's Lost: *A Retelling in Prose*

William Shakespeare's Macbeth: *A Retelling in Prose*

William Shakespeare's Measure for Measure: *A Retelling in Prose*

William Shakespeare's The Merchant of Venice: *A Retelling in Prose*

William Shakespeare's The Merry Wives of Windsor: *A Retelling in Prose*

William Shakespeare's A Midsummer Night's Dream: *A Retelling in Prose*

William Shakespeare's Much Ado About Nothing: *A Retelling in Prose*

William Shakespeare's Othello: *A Retelling in Prose*

William Shakespeare's Pericles, Prince of Tyre: *A Retelling in Prose*

William Shakespeare's Richard II: *A Retelling in Prose*

William Shakespeare's Richard III: *A Retelling in Prose*

William Shakespeare's Romeo and Juliet: *A Retelling in Prose*

William Shakespeare's The Taming of the Shrew: *A Retelling in Prose*

William Shakespeare's The Tempest: *A Retelling in Prose*

William Shakespeare's Timon of Athens: *A Retelling in Prose*

William Shakespeare's Titus Andronicus: *A Retelling in Prose*

William Shakespeare's Troilus and Cressida: *A Retelling in Prose*

William Shakespeare's Twelfth Night: *A Retelling in Prose*

William Shakespeare's The Two Gentlemen of Verona: *A Retelling in Prose*

William Shakespeare's The Two Noble Kinsmen: *A Retelling in Prose*

William Shakespeare's The Winter's Tale: *A Retelling in Prose*